ghost towns

Charlotte Amelia Poe

ISBN: 9798387587481

Copyright: Charlotte Amelia Poe.

All rights reserved.

For Mikey,

For being a constant in my life always, thank you. And thank you for all the ducks.

For Grace,

For being there from the first sentence to the last.

For Jay,

I cannot begin to sum it up. Just for being you. Endlessly.

"His heart is a suspended lute; As soon as you touch it, it resonates."

The Fall of the House of Usher, Edgar Allan Poe

PART I

Chapter One

@NME: *Where has Miles Montgomery gone and why don't we miss him? nme.com/news/miles-mont-…*

*

I drew a circle around you

Protecting, protecting, protecting

One day you pointed out

That I'd made you a crime scene

Teenage dream

Scrub the blood clean

Tell me you kept a piece of the evidence

My scarf in your closet

Keep it like innocence

- *This Is Not A Crime Scene, Miles Montgomery*

*

Miles Montgomery was in a bar in downtown Brooklyn drinking orange juice from a glass that probably cost more than his first car. He was tempted to smash it on the floor, to watch the ice cubes skid across the stained wood, just to see if they'd make him pay for it. Instead, he wrapped the cord of his hoodie around his finger and stared blankly at the drinks list above the bar: the artfully written chalk lettering standing out stark in pinks and blues against black.

The whole place reeked of money in an unavoidable way. Entry was exclusive, and privacy was guaranteed. Everyone was *someone*, and somehow that levelled the playing field a little. Nobody was going to take a photo or ask for an autograph. It was as close to anonymous as he could get.

He pulled out his phone, but there were no messages. He didn't know who he was waiting to hear from, really. Pretty much everyone he knew had been driven away by the blowback of his fame, the fucking cataclysm of an explosion that swept everyone in his orbit up and made them fodder for every clickbait article on the internet.

He made music, he was good at it, he made money from it. He wrote about what he knew and who he knew, and too little too late, realised what a mistake that had been. He'd laid himself utterly bare and now the vultures were circling. He was famous in a way he didn't really comprehend, in a way he didn't think anybody on the outside could ever comprehend. People loved him, people hated him, people wanted to marry him, people wanted to kill him. They played his songs at weddings; they played his songs at funerals.

He was inescapable.

So yeah, it was kind of fair that there were so many hit pieces out on him right now. His last record had landed awkwardly and he wasn't twenty five anymore, people wanted *more and better and new*, they wanted tours and festivals and meet and greets, they wanted a performance. They wanted him to be the person he was in their heads, different for each of them, but somehow, the perfect platonic ideal of Miles Montgomery: singer, songwriter, broken hearted and bitter, he'll love you right up until he writes a song about you and ruins your life.

The poor little rich boy routine was getting old, even to his ears, rattling around his brain as he tried to look for an escape route and couldn't find one. He'd tried to disappear, he hadn't done interviews, he hadn't made any public appearances, he hadn't tweeted or touched Instagram.

He was reeling, in a very real way. If *Spark*, his first record, had made him beloved, then *Grand Canyon*, his sixth record, had made him insufferable in the public's eyes. It was like a switch had been flipped. Enough, they'd said. Enough now.

And he could give them that. God knows he was trying. His contract was almost up and his record company was toddler-like in their demands to him. More, until the well was dry. Always more.

He didn't really feel like it.

Not anymore.

It used to be fun. It used to be so much fun. He'd gotten on stage and laughed out loud out of sheer exhilaration and the crowd had screamed back at him. He'd played until his fingers were sore and close to bleeding and it had felt like a privilege. He'd toured for two solid years playing the same songs, sure nobody would want to hear them again, and yet they had. They'd wanted.

But it was nastier now. The timelines of his last couple of breakups were messy, in a way that drew the vultures in closer to pick at the corpses. People stopped asking about the music, started asking about *him*, and *her*, and *why didn't anybody want to stay with him? Why was Miles so damn unlovable?*

Which felt a lot like kicking him when he was down, if he was honest. He'd made mistakes, because he was in his twenties and he was allowed to fucking do that, and yeah sometimes there'd been a pair of lips he shouldn't have kissed, and yeah maybe he'd slept around in a way that ruined that carefully curated image. Maybe he was ready to grow up, maybe he was older - maybe not wiser - but older and braver and trying to figure out what this all meant to him.

He should have ordered something other than orange juice, but that felt like a bad idea. This bar was the best kept secret in Brooklyn, but it wasn't impenetrable. If he got drunk, hell, if he even looked like he was drunk, it'd be all over the internet by morning.

Besides, he didn't like to drink. It hit a little too close to home, a little too close to the raw edges of his mother's death and the way his father had carried out bin bags that clanked a little too loudly. The sour smell of his breath and how they'd both tried to traverse those first blurry few months together, strangers to each other for the first time, both listing to opposite sides like they'd lost a limb each, unable to support each other, unable to do anything except bleed internally.

He pushed the hood of his hoodie down, ruffling a hand through hair that was getting too long. When he'd released his first album, it'd been buzzed short, but that hadn't been as marketable as the thick, carefully styled mop they'd made him grow instead, so here he was: dishevelled in a way that was supposed to be deliberate. Artistic. Like he was a real boy.

"Can I get you a drink?" A voice asked, and Miles turned to look. A man, attractive in the way everyone in the bar was, special, made mediocre even with designer stubble and heavy brows. Sea green eyes and a mouth that begged for sin. A body that was sculpted by hours in the gym every day. Miles had seen it all before. Had fucked it all before. It wasn't special, not anymore.

But –

Something about the man's face, open in a way that asked for nothing. The slight parting of that mouth, the uncertainty of the question. Miles felt his heart soften just enough to reply.

"I'm good, but thanks," he said, and gestured to his orange juice, where the ice cubes weren't really cubes anymore, rather weird little blobs sinking fast. The man nodded. Miles thought that'd be the end of it, but instead the man's face opened up a little more, and Miles could read a thousand emotions there, watching those eyes dart across his own face, searching for something.

"My friend sent me over here," the man said. "Jacob. Camden. He said we'd get on. And that he doesn't have your scarf. I don't know what that means."

Miles smiled, despite himself. Twenty two years old, and he and Jacob Camden had been a thing, Jacob, a British actor with an accent that had gradually slipped into something more Americanised over the years, who'd done the rounds on the BBC before breaking into Hollywood. They'd been young in a way Miles couldn't remember ever being now, and he'd loved Jacob, in a beautifully tortured way that wrapped him up in the other man, allowing him

to spew songs like they were falling out of him
after every argument, after the eventual breakup.

For years, they hadn't spoken, but they'd thawed
to each other again, remembering the good parts,
the heady rush of a first serious love, of moving
in together too quickly and picking out furniture.
Nights eating Chinese food in Jacob's London
apartment back before private jets and paparazzi.

"I found that scarf the day after the song came
out," Miles said. "And I've told him that a
thousand times. He just likes to – needle me
with it, because I hated his dumb scarves.
Always said New York was too cold for him.
He's from fucking England, the country where it
rains," Miles rolled his eyes. "He sent you over
here to say that?"

"I'm Alexander," the man – Alexander, said.
"He told me to come over here because he
knows you, and he knows me, and this is a
pretty blatant attempt at matchmaking. And this
is going to sound really shitty, but if you could
just pretend to go along with it I'd owe you
one."

"You didn't ask me my name," Miles said. It
bothered him, in some indefinable way. Like he
was public property to the point where he
couldn't even be addressed.

"Miles," Alexander said, and Miles had to take a second to acknowledge how his name sounded on Alexander's tongue, normally it sounded too short, or too abrupt, but Alexander somehow made it last an age, like it actually mattered. It wasn't being screamed, it wasn't for attention, it was just his name. How long had that been? "Miles, everybody knows who you are. You're Miles Montgomery."

"You're something famous too," Miles pointed out. "Or famous-adjacent. Otherwise they wouldn't let you in here."

"Not in a way that matters, believe me. I don't – I try not to get too involved. It's abstract, and that sounds pretentious, but it is. It's money, and it's using my body to get more money. More than I need, probably. I know I'm lucky, and I know I have maybe five years before I don't get to do this anymore. I can't imagine what it's like to be you, not even close. The entitlement that you must – people want you, all the time, right? Like you're painted in gold leaf and it might just rub off on them. I don't feel like that. And that sounds like a line. But really. I don't date. I don't fuck. I don't really talk to people I don't know. I'm talking to you because my friends think I need to get back on the horse, and they don't seem to realise that horse has been dead and buried for over a decade. So I'm asking you if I can leave with you, and that's all. I have an Uber booked, it's about," Alexander checks his phone, "seven minutes away. I'm not asking you to come home with me. I just need to be seen to be trying. And I hate it. But I need to pretend to be a normal fucking human for one night, and maybe then my friends will stop."

Miles was a little taken aback. He got the feeling Alexander wasn't a man for big speeches or a lot of words all at once.

"You need a story to tell," Miles said carefully.

Alexander nodded. "I hear you're the best at them."

"Not in a way that matters," Miles said, echoing Alexander's earlier sentiment.

"I don't believe that," Alexander said, and seemed to mean it.

Miles pushed his orange juice away, and scraped his chair back. Alexander looked a little surprised, like he hadn't expected this to actually work.

"How long on that Uber?" Miles asked. Alexander checked his phone.

"Still seven minutes. God, I hate Brooklyn."

"You want to wait outside? It might add credence to the whole thing if we disappear off together," Miles asked.

Alexander glanced over to a corner table, and Miles followed his gaze, making out the distinct visage of Jacob sitting there. Jacob raised a lazy hand in greeting, and smiled crookedly, the way he always smiled. There was a song about that.

"We could wait outside," Alexander said. "How are you getting home, though? Are you safe?"

Miles pulled his hood up and slid a pair of thick glasses out from the pocket at the front. It was stupid that the Clark Kent/Superman trick worked, but take away the hair, distort his features just enough, and he was suddenly invisible, just another Brooklyn hipster.

"I live close," he said. "Literally, ten minutes away. I shouldn't tell you that, but I get the feeling you're not going to tell anybody. And hey, I'll know it was you if it gets out."

"I'm a ways out," Alexander said, "still Brooklyn, but only just. I wanted more space, and I couldn't justify the prices. I guess you don't have to worry about that." He paused, and shook his head. Miles felt a little taken aback. Alexander bit his lip and looked rueful. "Sorry, that was shitty. I just mean - I don't know what I mean. You're kind of next level."

"It's okay. It's overwhelming, right? I'm overwhelming. I'm sort of used to it."

"I don't like that you're used to it," Alexander said, and his face opened up a little more, and Miles marvelled at it, because from a distance Alexander had to be the kind of man who wore expressionless like armour, but up close, he was all emotion.

"I don't either," Miles said, and shrugged. "I'm trying not to be. Overwhelming. But I'm a spark, right? That used to mean something different to me. Now I know exactly what it means. I burn things."

"But they," and Alexander didn't need to explain what he means by *they*. They both know, in that unspoken way. "They burn you down just the same."

"Burn your idols, right?" Miles said.

"Kill your heroes," Alexander replied, and Miles nudged a shoulder against him.

"How come you get it? Where have you been?" Miles asked. "Jacob never mentioned you. Shit, do you need to say goodbye to him?"

"Fuck him, he put us both in an awkward situation," Alexander said, leaning slightly into Miles' touch.

"Didn't you listen to my songs? I did that already," Miles said, and smirked to himself, because he'd only said it to see Alexander's reaction, which was a fabulous display of eyebrow pyrotechnics.

"I don't believe everything I hear," Alexander said after recovering, cheeks flushed a little pink as they stepped outside.

"A lot of it's true, turns out. More than I'd like."

"There are different types of truth. At least you get to sing yours."

"I guess. It just – gets old, y'know? Reading about myself, and I know I shouldn't, but I do, because I'm a human being with access to Google, of course I'm going to read it. But it's half-truths and almosts and it's messy. It's always messy. They lay it out in black and white, bullet points, you know? Graphics, someone gets paid to make graphics about my love life. It's all there and I'm reading it and I almost believe it. Because when so many people are saying it's real, it has to be, right?" Miles let out a long sigh. Alexander bumped his shoulder, and the backs of their hands nudged together for one electric second.

They made their way down the street, to where Alexander had told the Uber to pick him up. It was nice, to find someone who really understood the bullshit of it all. Even if he never saw Alexander again, it was nice to have been able to have this conversation. He'd needed it.

"What would you like them to say?" Alexander asked into the quiet.

Miles thought for a minute.

"Nothing. No, because you don't get on stage, you don't write songs if you want nothing back, do you? I don't know, anymore. I was seventeen years old when I signed that contract. I signed away so much more than I realised. I've made six albums and people hate me. What do I want them to say? That I was good, maybe? Not in the way they'll say after I die, but now. I want to hear it now. All the nice shit they say at funerals that they'd never say to your face. I want that. Not lies, but just - tell me something real. Something that hasn't been distorted. Something that isn't mirror universe. But yeah, tell me I've done something worthwhile. That all of this," Miles waved a hand in the air in front of him, "that all of this was worth something."

Alexander looked at him for a long time, long enough that Miles had to look away, because it felt like he was being stripped bare. Finally, he felt Alexander look down at his phone, then up at a black car that was pulling in to the curb.

"That you?" Miles asked, nodding at the Nissan.

"Yeah."

Alexander put his hand on the door handle, nodding to the driver. Miles reached out and had to stop himself from grabbing Alexander's wrist, the aborted movement catching Alexander's attention. He looked back at Miles.

"If I asked you if I could get in that car with you, what would you say?" Miles asked, and Alexander closed off, just a little, a little sadder, a little older, suddenly.

"I'd say no," he said simply, when it didn't feel simple at all.

"It's bad, isn't it? The reason you're saying no," Miles said, because it was, wasn't it, it had to be.

Evenings like this didn't end with goodbyes and Alexander driving away. The whole time, Alexander had been present but slightly removed, and Miles had seen it before, in a thousand different ways, normally in the eyes of young women, but sometimes men, too. His stomach churned.

"Does that help? If it is?" Alexander asked quietly, looking down at his feet.

"Not really. No. Not at all, actually. I don't know why I said it," Miles managed, wanting to take it back, close Pandora's box, stuff the knowledge away. Someone had hurt Alexander. And for some reason, that made Miles want to cry.

"It's bad," Alexander said, curt, and it would have been brusque, but it couldn't be, because despite the way he forced the words out, they still sounded small.

"I'm sorry," Miles said, because what the fuck else could he say? There weren't words, there never were. This industry, all of it, was built on the backs of people like Alexander. Miles didn't need the specifics to know exactly the burden Alexander carried. The reason he was saying no.

"Huh," Alexander said, surprising Miles, and he looked right at Miles then, those eyes that seemed to shift colour with the light looking almost grey, somehow.

"What?" Miles asked, because Alexander's face was wide open now, years stripped away, and Miles could write an entire album about that transformation, those desperate few seconds.

"I don't think anyone's ever apologised for it before," Alexander said, and seemed to struggle with himself for a few seconds, his eyebrows drawing close, before reaching out and rubbing a thumb over Miles' knuckles. It felt like a gift, given carefully, without want for reciprocation.

He pulled the car door open, and got inside. Miles watched him get driven away, further and further out of Miles' life, until the car turned the corner and was gone.

Miles stood for a long time, bumped by the occasional passer-by. Then, he turned on his heel and headed home, the beginnings of a headache forming behind his right eye, his knuckles burning white hot where Alexander had touched them.

Chapter Two

BUZZFEED: WHO THE F#!K IS MILES MONTGOMERY AND WHY SHOULD WE CARE?

"One topic wonder and all round conversation stopper, you wouldn't want to invite Miles Montgomery to your party. Listening to his albums, you wonder if he ever does anything other than complain. And yet, he's led a charmed life, by all accounts. And his headboard carries some pretty impressive tallies. And you know what? It's boring. It's boring every time he trends on Twitter and every time he prances around looking for attention. Always the victim, never to blame, that's how all the songs go. Maybe it's time we stopped paying attention to Miles Montgomery."

*

"Talk about a saviour complex

I knelt down at your altar

And lit a candle for all the words you didn't say

Chasing gods at the bottom of bottles

The hotel mini-bar ran dry

And you fell asleep with all my I love yous falling on deaf ears

- This Has To (Be The Last Time), Miles Montgomery

*

Miles woke up to the beam of light falling across his face where he hadn't shut his blinds all the way the night before and felt like a cliché. Every opening scene to every movie ever. He rolled over in the big, empty bed with its perfect white sheets and perfect fluffed pillows, all but one, anyway, one was flat and blue and smelt like home, like twenty years ago and childhood. It was one of the secrets nobody knew about him, one of the things that could be traded for money or influence. He kept it under the bed when people visited. He didn't need to give away that kind of leverage.

He thought back to the night before, to getting home and tipping back a couple of painkillers before passing out, bleary thoughts of Alexander and the conversation they'd had echoing through his head. It felt like it should be capitalised. *The Conversation*. Like it had been more than just words, it had been an understanding.

Miles was too jaded to believe in fate, or kismet, or any of the other words he liked to use in his songs. They were lovely words, but they weren't real. Alexander had been real though, hadn't he? In a damaged, open wound kind of a way, Alexander had been the most real thing in Miles' life for a very long time.

And he'd disappeared. He'd been written out of the story. And Miles could ask Jacob for his number, Miles could be *That Guy*, but there was something about Alexander that reminded him of a cornered animal, the way he'd blurted out that he'd needed Miles' help, the way he'd said that it had been bad.

Miles knew *bad* in specific ways, death and alcohol and teeth clenching loneliness and being ripped to shreds online. But he got the feeling that Alexander's bad was different, not worse, because it was never going to be a competition, but enough to hollow out a nasty little niche inside of him and eat away at him until it bled all over him, until everyone could see.

Miles knew about bleeding out, about bleeding out publicly. He knew how to hide it. He knew Alexander was hiding it well, and he ached for the man, because he'd seen glimpses of what was beneath the surface. Behind that shiny perfect façade that went a long way in this city, but not far enough that Miles couldn't help but want to reach out.

Alexander had Jacob though, and for all their history, Miles loved Jacob in a way that he couldn't put into words, and he'd tried – goddamn he'd tried. Two albums of trying, always fumbling the landing, and now, texts and DMs and late night phone calls when neither of them had anything else to do. He wasn't sure if they were friends or just two people in the same boat, two people bound together because Miles had made a choice, nearly seven years ago, to write Jacob into the narrative of his life.

Jacob blamed him for a long time for that. Blamed him for the talk show questions and for the Personal Life section on his Wikipedia page. Blamed him three years ago when they'd fucked because they'd needed it in that moment, in the same bar by mistake too close to closing and with a bathroom door with a lock that offered just enough privacy to lead to bad decisions.

After that though, it fell away, the blame, the animosity, the subtle passive aggressive remarks. It worked better when they were a united front, and Jacob was a household name now and he understood it better now, understood the way people wanted to burrow under Miles' skin and set up camp there.

Miles had been there when Jacob had received his first death threat to his home address. Miles had helped him pick out the best security system money could buy. Miles had gone with him to the police station to hand the letter in, careful to seal it in a ziploc bag and careful that only Jacob had touched it.

Sheriff's son, after all.

And then Miles had spent the night in Jacob's living room with him, a blanket fort strewn across the furniture, and an aluminium baseball bat a few feet away. It had solidified something, then.

Jacob had been there when Miles' reputation had started to fall apart around him. When being seen with Miles meant taking a bullet meant for him. Jacob had offered him, time and time again, the use of his London apartment if Miles needed to get away.

It was so fucking tempting.

So maybe Jacob knew Alexander in the same way Jacob knew Miles. Bone deep and blood and guts, all the messy stuff. The real stuff.

Maybe last night hadn't been the set up Alexander had thought it had been.

Jacob said that Miles was smart, but in a very roundabout way. Emotionally intelligent, but stupid with it. Jacob was more stable, but prone to hot headedness. They knew each other's weak spots because they'd loved those same vulnerable places, lavished praise upon them.

Did Jacob know Alexander's weak spots too? Why had Jacob never mentioned Alexander before? Had that been an act of protection? From Miles, or from who the media thought Miles was? What had changed?

There was a thought at the back of his mind, fluttering and desperate, that allowed him to hope that maybe Alexander had asked about Miles, somewhere along the line. And that Jacob had answered. And Jacob was honest, brutally honest in that very British way, and maybe Alexander had seen something in Miles that had allowed him to trust.

The idea took flight and nested on the branches of Miles' consciousness. He got the feeling Alexander didn't trust very easily.

His phone buzzed, and he rolled over to grab it, wincing when he saw the time.

JACOB: *So Alexander wants your number, you cool?*

JACOB: *He thinks you're interesting. I honestly thought he had better taste. How do you tell your friend that he is so deeply, deeply misguided?*

MILES: *Give him my number, sure.*

MILES: *How to tell someone they're not funny? Your dialogue is really lacking without a script.*

JACOB: *You wound me, Montgomery. Alexander says hey. If you two get married, I want to be your flower girl.*

MILES: *England called, they want you to fuck off home.*

JACOB: *You love me.*

MILES: *Lies and slander.*

Miles let out a shuddering breath. Alexander had asked for his number. That meant something, right? Alexander hadn't disappeared out of his life. Alexander might even want to be *in* his life.

He pressed the back of his hand over his eyes, and lay there for a moment, letting it be dark.

Was he going to drag Alexander down? Would he let himself do that? Because falling into Miles Montgomery's orbit? That was a fucking death wish. And Alexander was already walking wounded.

*

Miles did get out of bed eventually, even if it was closer to afternoon than he'd have liked to admit. His brain itched in the way it did when a new song was forming, and he had to stop himself from opening his Notes app and tapping out a few lines. He didn't know why he stopped himself – well, no, that was a lie. He knew exactly why. He wanted to write about Alexander.

Alexander, who presumably had his number now, unless Jacob was that much of a dick.

It felt like breaking some kind of unspoken vow to put any of what they'd talked about into words, no matter how well he disguised them with metaphors and storytelling. People would know, because people always knew. He couldn't do that without Alexander's permission. He wasn't sure he could do it *with* Alexander's permission. He was kind of done with fucking up other people's lives because his career depended on it.

As if sensing his discomfort, his phone rang, the shrill personal ringtone he'd assigned to his manager and close friend forged through fire, Jennifer. She had a sixth sense for when he was doubting himself, it seemed, and this was no different, apparently. She always knew when to catch him and reel him back in.

"Jennifer," he greeted her, because they'd known each other long enough to skip the pleasantries.

"Montgomery," she replied, slightly clipped like she'd sharpened her accent on purpose. Perhaps she had.

"What do they want?" Miles asked, because it was always something. She never rang him with good news. The day she did, he'd run for the nearest bunker, or check to see if hell had frozen over. Something suitably dramatic.

"A video for *Americana*. Filmed within the next two weeks, preferably. They have a director, you've worked with him before, you hate him, he hates you, it'll be a cinematic masterpiece, you know how it goes."

Miles could imagine her waving her hand idly, to signal at the level of bullshit she had to deal with.

"This is a power play," Miles said.

"Essentially," she confirmed. "You're the highest bidder for your masters and they'll give you them if you round out this album. You play this right and you get everything you wanted. It won't be cheap, but you'll own your music and you can leave this contract behind."

"So generous of them. So where are we on the chessboard?" Miles asked.

"We can't get them cheaper, but we can get them. And they won't seek a second contract. You'll be a free agent. I hear Universal's interested. They've been making some noise, off the record."

"It can't be that easy," Miles said, suspicious. "What's the catch?"

Jennifer sighed. "Your bid is significantly higher than the others, and more than a couple of bidders have dropped out. Legally, you have to pay what you've offered, even though the value has dropped. People don't want to be associated with you right now. This is good, though. Universal can see through it. That's what you want."

"So one music video and I'm done? They don't want a tour?" Miles checked.

"They don't think you could sell one. Have you Googled yourself recently? It's bad, Miles."

It must be, because she never used his first name.

"You're haemorrhaging right now, Montgomery. Which works in your favour. Universal is asking less of you, and whilst they're offering less money with it, it's a safer bet. You've got everyone right where you want them. You play this right, you take the king."

Miles hummed to himself. He could live with that. It wasn't good to hear, but it was what he'd worked towards for a long time, owning his masters, something he'd given up when he'd signed that contract at seventeen, being free of the record label he was signed with. No more tours. Just one music video. He could do that.

"So what's the aesthetic?" He asked, and knew Jennifer would jump topics with him.

"Think Springsteen. Forget New York, this is rural New Jersey. Barns and fields and corn. They're taking it very literally. A love story gone wrong. A boy from the wrong side of the tracks and you. They're casting. I think they're trying to bury you."

Americana had been Miles' reckoning with his own place in American pop culture, and it had drawn a lot of criticism for being too honest, too brutal. He could see how they would make this a funeral.

He had a thought. It was stupid, perhaps, but it could make this whole thing more tolerable.

"They're casting?" He asked, to be sure.

"Yes," Jennifer replied, suspicious.

"How much power do I have over that?" Miles asked carefully.

"Depends who you're thinking of."

"If I give you a name, can you do this for me? I'll owe you one," Miles asked, and knew exactly how much he'd owe her for this.

"You owe me everything. I can give you twelve hours. Don't make me regret this."

"You won't," Miles promised, and hoped he could keep it.

"Already am," Jennifer said, and hung up. The silence stretched for a long minute before Miles stared at his phone and willed it to chime.

UNKNOWN NUMBER: *This is Alexander.*

Sometimes the universe had perfect timing. Miles made a decision he hoped he wouldn't regret. He tapped out a message and pressed Send.

MILES: *Not to be presumptuous, but how do you feel about being in a music video?*

Chapter Three

@jacobcamden: Americans have no taste (won't watch University Challenge with me)

@MilesMontgomery: @jacobcamden starter for ten why are you so pretentious?

*

"Jacob said you'd have questions," Alexander's voice comes clear and warm over the phone line, not five minutes after Miles sent the text. Miles didn't know what he'd been expecting, but not this. "He said you could be impulsive."

"That's why you agreed to approach me, right?" Miles asked. "Last night."

Alexander is silent for a few seconds. "Not just that, no."

"Oh. Well. Sorry? Am I apologising here? I feel like I should be apologising but I'm not sure what for."

"Don't apologise. You haven't done anything wrong. I'm just – surprised. You're serious about the music video?" Alexander asked.

Miles blew out a long breath.

"It's going to suck. But I thought – god this sounds stupid now because I barely know you at all, but I thought it might suck less if you were there. I liked talking to you. I wasn't going to – chase you or anything. Honestly. But Jacob texted and said you wanted my number and – it didn't feel so one-sided anymore."

"Are there sides to this?" Alexander asked.

"I don't know. I think there could be," Miles replied honestly.

"I don't date. I told you that. Please don't turn this into something it isn't. I don't do messy," Alexander said and it hit the back of Miles' throat and sat there, heavy.

So many people, so many, called Miles messy. He knew he was, in a thousand different ways. But it still hurt to hear.

"I'm not trying to date you," Miles said honestly, still hurting. "And yeah, I try not to do messy either. Messy sucks. Google me. You know messy sucks for me. I just thought – I don't have many friends. I could really, really use a friend. I know I have this reputation for dating anything that moves but sometimes I just need somebody. And maybe I got it into my head last night that you understood that. And maybe, god, maybe I thought you might need that too."

Alexander was quiet for so long Miles had to check the call hadn't dropped.

"I don't trust easy," Alexander said eventually. "It's to my deficit, but I had to learn the hard way, you know? And I know you do know. The way you looked at me last night, I'm not stupid. You said you were sorry. So, you know. I don't trust – people don't always say what they really want. And sometimes people look at me and they want me. I'm not saying that to be vain, it's what my career is based on. I'm a model. Alexander Raine, look me up. Or don't. I'm not proud of it. But I got stuck in this. I know what people want from me. It's hard to believe you'd want something different."

Miles' brain ran up to a dozen sentences and held them all tight on his tongue before he replied.

I got stuck in this.

How long had Miles felt stuck for? Years, now. He had at least two Spotify playlists dedicated to pro-union songs and workers' rebellions. On a private account, obviously. He listened *to Blood On The Risers* and related to it. Every day he jumped and wondered if his parachute would work.

Alexander didn't want messy. Miles didn't want messy either. So maybe Miles had thought there had been a moment between them the night before when Alexander had rubbed his thumb over Miles' knuckles. It was Miles' job to read into shit like that. Alexander couldn't have foreseen Miles seeing it for more than it was.

It still felt like something though, but Miles wasn't going to push. He wouldn't do that to Alexander. Maybe Alexander *had* wanted it to mean more, but that didn't mean he owed anything to Miles now.

"I don't want anything you don't want," Miles said after what felt like too long. "I know that sounds disingenuous, or like a lie. I wouldn't believe it if someone said it to me, either. You don't have to be in the music video. It just seemed like a good fit. And maybe there was a part of me that wanted to see you again. And maybe I overstepped. No, I did. I overstepped and I'm sorry. I want us to be equals and I forget sometimes how difficult that can be for people around me. That sounds so big headed but I think you get it, right? I told you I burn things. That wasn't a lie."

"They burn you at the stake every day, Miles," Alexander said, and Miles still marvelled at the way Alexander said his name, like it was a brand new word to Miles' ears. He had to stop thinking like that, but he couldn't. His hamartia, that pesky fatal flaw, was a streak of stubborn romanticism that threatened to destroy him every step of the way. "You didn't overstep. Tell me about the video."

"Well, it's New Jersey, so it'll probably be on location, which is a special kind of hell they've decided upon for me. So I am asking you to come to New Jersey for me. Which could be a deal breaker, I know. Springsteen vibes. It's for *Americana*. I don't know if you've heard it, but apparently they're leaning into it pretty heavily."

"They're releasing *Americana*?" Alexander asked, and Miles was surprised to note that Alexander seemed a little shocked. So it wasn't just Miles that felt like this was an attempt to ruin him. Alexander said as much in the next sentence. "People hate that song, Miles."

"I know. Believe me, I know. And you know what's funny? It only makes me like it more. It's the end of an era and if this is how I leave this whole thing behind me, then fine. It's funny, I told you about what I'd want them to say about me after I died. Guess I'm going to find out, huh."

"You're not going to die, Miles. You're going to make more music," Alexander said softly. Miles tapped his fingers against his knee, one, two, three, before replying.

"It's an ending. Endings always mean something," he said.

"Sometimes it's good that things end. It means you get to be free of them. You don't sound – I'm sorry to say this, but you don't sound very happy with your life right now. So maybe this is a good thing," Alexander said.

"It is a good thing," Miles agreed. "It's just… I didn't think I'd agree to dig my own grave, is all."

"I'll do the video," Alexander said abruptly. "Send me a contract, I'll give you my agent's details. I'll do it."

The sudden agreement spun Miles' head a little. He couldn't parse it for a moment.

"I mean, yeah, but why?" He said, dumbly.

"Because I want to take you out to dinner after. Call it a wake if you want, you're pretentious enough to do that, right?" Alexander paused, and Miles couldn't help but bark out a laugh. "If it's going to suck that much, I want you to have something to look forward to. I'll find some sleazy diner and we'll toast to whatever comes next with chocolate milkshakes. I know how easy it could be to spiral, so, what if I didn't let you?"

"Why would you do that?" Miles still didn't understand.

"Because you said you needed a friend. I'm not – I'm not good for much in this world. But I can be that," Alexander said, and it nearly broke Miles' heart to hear.

"I think you're more than you realise," Miles said gently.

"Miles," Alexander said, "don't get messy."

The call ended, and Miles slumped heavier into the couch. His mind whirred up, cogs already turning, steaming, screeching.

He programmed Alexander's number into his phone and stared at the contact information for a long time.

Alexander was offering a lifeline. And he didn't have to do that. Miles just had to keep his feelings separate, as muddled as they were. Alexander didn't want more than he was offering, and that was fine. Miles wasn't sure he could accept any more than that right now anyway.

No. That was a lie. Miles already knew he'd accept anything Alexander offered him.

Don't get messy.

Fuck.

He texted Alexander's name to Jennifer, not Googling him beforehand. That didn't feel fair to Alexander. Half an hour later, Jennifer texted back.

JENNIFER: *He's on board.*

*

"I draped myself in you

Careful so the stars and stripes shone through

Small town boy with enough grit to survive

Maybe I did have stars in my eyes

But you snuffed them out

> *I'm empty to the core*
>
> *I'm trying to tell you*
>
> *I'm not your American boy anymore."*
>
> *- Americana, Miles Montgomery*

*

MILES: *So how do you know Jacob?*

ALEXANDER: *Same magazine shoot, he stood out.*

MILES: *Oooooooh so he was complaining.*

ALEXANDER: *He has opinions about eyeliner brands I didn't know a person could have.*

*

ALEXANDER: *Have you Googled me yet?*

MILES: *No, actually.*

ALEXANDER: *I don't mind if you do.*

MILES: *Yeah, but still.*

MILES: *I'd rather get to know you by actually talking to you. Not reading about you.*

ALEXANDER: *You want to get to know me?*

MILES: *I thought I'd kinda made that clear, but yeah.*

ALEXANDER: *Just surprises me, is all.*

MILES: *Why?*

ALEXANDER: *People don't normally think I have anything worth listening to to say.*

ALEXANDER: *They don't pay models to talk, you know.*

MILES: *I'm sorry people treat you like that. Cats or dogs?*

MILES: *Wait! No! Wolves or foxes?*

ALEXANDER: *Foxes.*

MILES: *I mean, you're wrong, but I'd love to hear your reasoning.*

*

"I refuse to let this stand!" Miles said into the phone, mock angry. He knew Alexander must be raising his eyebrows as he listened, taken aback by the impromptu call.

"Miles Montgomery has an opinion and suddenly everyone has to hear about it," Alexander drawled, and Miles sort of loved that they'd gotten to this stage in their – whatever they had, friendship? Alexander had come around to mocking him really quickly, quickly enough that Miles could only presume Jacob's bad influence, if he was honest. He was Miles *fucking* Montgomery, he deserved some respect. Alexander staunchly refused to give it though, and Miles' heart grew three sizes every time Alexander full-named him. It always meant trouble. In the best way.

"I don't know what lies Jacob has been telling you but American chocolate is not superior to English chocolate. He's literally lying to you. For attention, probably, you know what actors are like. God, when we were dating he would import it and I could have lived off it. He just doesn't want to share his stash, that's what it is, you know. He's lying to protect himself. To protect his horrible chocolate-hoarding ways," Miles finished in a huff.

"Uh huh, uh huh," Alexander said, and Miles waited for the punch line. Alexander thought he was funny. (Miles thought Alexander was funny, if he was honest, but he would never tell the man that.) "And you're saying that on the record? We can quote you on that? Camden's Tragic Chocolate Addiction?"

"You're such an asshole. I don't know why I talk to you," Miles complained, but couldn't help but smile. Alexander could be playful when he wanted to, and Miles loved bringing it out of him. He'd sort of forgotten that people could have so many multitudes, and Alexander was as multi-faceted as they came. Their conversations could boomerang from the serious to the mundane, and back again all in a few sentences. It wasn't hard work. Miles had kind of expected it would be, given his initial feelings towards Alexander, but a week and a half of near constant communication with him had given the first night they'd met an air of distance, like it was a folk story Miles had heard and not something that had actually happened to him.

It wasn't messy. It was just nice.

Nice wasn't a word Miles could use in a song, because it felt too wishy-washy, like it couldn't make is mind up enough to be *great* or *amazing*. And Alexander was both of those things as well. But he was also nice. And sometimes, Miles needed nice.

But Alexander was an asshole, too.

"You talk to me because I'm going to be playing your diamond in the rough boyfriend in your music video next week, and then I'm going to buy you burgers. Because your life is so difficult," Alexander snarked back. Miles rolled his eyes, even though Alexander couldn't see him.

"Well they must have miscast you because you seem to have been up for the role of douchecanoe and wandered into the wrong room."

"A wordsmith, a poet, the greatest lyricist of our time."

"Fuck off, nerd," Miles said without heat. Alexander was a total nerd, he'd found out, about so many things. Miles knew Alexander had paused nature documentaries to talk to him before. Miles would know David Attenborough's voice anywhere. Alexander watched history documentaries *for fun*.

"Grammy award winning, first dance shit," Alexander continued.

"I'll be your first dance," Miles threatened nonsensically.

"Yeah, I doubt it, for so many reasons," Alexander replied, and the humour was there, but some of the levity had vanished from his voice.

It clicked in Miles' head violently.

"You don't date, so, no getting married, huh," Miles said dumbly.

"That's how it tends to go, yeah," Alexander said softly, and sighed. "That is how it tends to go."

"Would you even want that, though? To get married? Not everybody needs to pair off."

"Is it stupid that I do want that? Despite everything, if it was the right person. Maybe it wouldn't be so bad," Alexander said, voice still soft. Like he was confessing a secret. Maybe he was.

"It's not supposed to be bad at all, you know? It's not something you're supposed to get through. It's supposed to be fun. My parents – " Miles stopped himself, already imagining the headline. But no, he trusted Alexander. Perhaps more than he should. "My parents had fun. Before my mom died. They laughed so much. It was such – such a happy household. I mean, there must have been bad bits, but I remember it being so happy. Almost like it couldn't have been real. And then it wasn't. But for eight years of my life, I got to live in that world, so I think. The right person, I think that's everything."

"What if there isn't a right person?" Alexander asked, and the question was so simple it sounded almost childish, but so full of hope. Miles couldn't bring himself to dash it if he wanted to.

"Just because you have misguided opinions on chocolate, and you're a massive nerd, and an asshole, and your face is weirdly symmetrical, doesn't mean they're not out there," Miles said, knowing that's not what he meant at all.

"They'd have to put up with more than that," Alexander said quietly, almost breathing the words out.

"The right person would, though," Miles said, because it was obvious.

"Hmm."

*

MILES: *I always get ants in my pants the night before a video shoot. ADHD kid turned ADHD adult, ya know? I start thinking about all the shit I'm going to have to do, and how long the days are going to be, and makeup and all that. And then I have nightmares where I turn up and I can't remember the lyrics to the song. I don't even have to sing it, just mime, but still. Ants. In. Pants.*

ALEXANDER: *Disgusting. I should tell PETA.*

MILES: *Alexander Raine, counsellor to the stars.*

ALEXANDER: *Bitch, pay me.*

Chapter Four

@MilesMontgomery

ARE YOU SURE YOU WANT TO DEACTIVATE YOUR ACCOUNT?

YES / NO

*

Miles hated waking up early for video shoots. He hated having to be driven for what felt like hours to get to whatever obscure location someone he'd never met had chosen for him. He hated that he'd drank three coffees and his left eye was twitching in a way that would make the makeup artists grumpy at him.

But he would get to see Alexander. So maybe, he thought as he breathed in the New Jersey air, staring at the expanse of fields and the ramshackle barn behind him, at the farm machinery Miles guessed he or Alexander would be draping themselves over later, at the claw footed bathtub he hoped to god they had hot water for, maybe it wouldn't be completely terrible. He stifled a yawn behind his coffee cup and blinked his eyes clear. People were running around everywhere, there was a lot of yelling, everyone was very frantic, a lot of jobs depended on him being on his best behaviour. Him getting his masters back depended on his best behaviour.

A car crunched up behind him, and the next thing he knew, footsteps were approaching and he heard his name spoken in that unmistakeable way.

"Miles," Alexander said warmly, and Miles turned, and lifted his arms to hug him before faltering. Alexander looked bemused, a little, and Miles berated himself for treating him with kid gloves.

"Do we hug?" Alexander asked. "Is that a thing we do?"

"Do you *want* a hug?" Miles replied, and suddenly Alexander was on the back foot, and Miles could practically see his brain trying to form a witty response. Finally, Alexander shrugged and smiled.

"I guess I do," he said simply, and somehow that meant more than anything funny he could have said.

Miles closed the gap between them and wrapped his arms around Alexander's waist, hands moving up so that they rested gently just below Alexander's shoulder blades. It wasn't the kind of hug friends gave each other. Miles expected Alexander to pull away, but instead he seemed to sink into it, resting his nose against the crook of Miles' neck. Miles could swear Alexander breathed him in.

They parted reluctantly and Alexander looked Miles up and down.

"You look like shit," he said, and Miles scowled.

"It's like, five in the morning, fuck off. We don't all roll out of bed looking like underwear models."

"I was an underwear model, so," Alexander said, eyes lighting up.

"Oh, well we've all been underwear models," Miles said and waved a hand airily, "but have you ever been voted Most Hated Celebrity two years running? No. So I win."

"I don't think that's a prize I want," Alexander said. "I've seen your photo shoots, you work out."

"Reluctantly, and with an intense phobia of being seen doing so, yes," Miles acknowledged. "I have like, an allergic reaction afterwards, hives and shit. It's gross."

"Oh, you reminded me," Alexander said, and reached into his pocket and pulled out a blister packet of pills. He popped two out, before dry swallowing them. "Allergies. Countryside, you know." He didn't meet Miles' eyes, seeming to want to look anywhere but directly at Miles.

For the first time, Miles didn't quite believe him. Miles reluctantly shrugged it off. It was too early for thinking too deeply.

"Is there a good reason there's a bathtub?" Alexander asked, looking around properly for the first time.

"Is there ever a good reason for a bathtub?" Miles replied dryly. "One or both of us is going to get submerged in water that is slightly too cold and end up feeling vaguely clammy for the rest of the day. Show business." He did jazz hands to emphasise his point.

"Not loving that," Alexander said.

Someone called Miles' name and Miles sighed and wanted nothing more than to ignore it. He just wanted to spend the day talking to Alexander.

"I think they want you in makeup," Alexander said, nodding to the person trying to get Miles' attention.

"The amount I do not want to do this," Miles whined.

"Want me to come with?" Alexander asked. "They can do me at the same time, I can keep you company."

"You're an angel, Alexander Raine," Miles breathed, and smiled.

"Please tell me you have a regular amount of opinions about eyeliner," Alexander grinned, and Miles couldn't help but grin back.

"Other than wishing I could do winged eyeliner just to prove a point? I'm entirely neutral," Miles said.

"That sounds like a story," Alexander said, prompting Miles as they started to walk towards a trailer.

So Miles launched into a brief recap of his adventures with liquid eyeliner and a very unsteady hand, warmed by Alexander's small noises of acknowledgement.

*

"I guess you're used to this, huh?" Miles said, taking in how relaxed Alexander was, slumped down in the makeup chair beside Miles, meeting his eyes in the big mirror.

"Close your eyes," the makeup artist working on Miles said, and he obliged, feeling the sweep of pencil eyeliner along his lashes.

"It goes with the job," Alexander said, and it was weird to hear his voice in the dark of closed eyes. Miles could feel the makeup artist pull back and opened his eyes again. He looked at Alexander in the mirror, as the hair stylist did something complicated to Alexander's hair to make it look effortless, like he'd just rolled out of bed.

"Your eyes are really brown," Alexander commented, meeting Miles' eyes again and holding the gaze. He quirked a smile and Miles couldn't help but watch himself blush in response.

"They like putting eyeliner on me," Miles said, aiming for flippant and failing.

"You're like goddamn Bambi," Alexander said, and Miles shot him a side glance. He was slouched more now, and Miles thought back to the pills he'd seen Alexander take about twenty minutes before – what colour had they been again, blue? - and thought *oh, right*.

"You're weirdly chill," he said, trying to sound nonchalant.

Alexander shrugged. "I'm used to this."

Miles was a big believer in listening when things started to ping his uncanny radar, and it was pinging big time. He couldn't say anything, not here, but watching Alexander's eyes slide half shut with the stylist's hands in his hair made Miles uncomfortable.

"Are you tired?" He asked, and Alexander shrugged again.

"I'll be fine in about fifteen minutes, guess the early start is hitting me. Just keep talking to me."

Miles chewed at his bottom lip, and let the makeup artist pluck away a few stray eyebrow hairs. He watched Alexander out of the corner of his eye, trying to remember what the pills had looked like. He thought they could have been blue, but he wasn't sure. It had been too quick. Still, his dad had taught him never to disregard evidence.

"I think you're done, honey. And you might want to wake your friend, they'll be wanting him for wardrobe," the makeup artist said, and Miles looked at where Alexander's eyes had drooped shut, highlighting the subtle browns and purples they'd used on his eyelids to bring out the green of his mercurial eyes.

Miles reached out a hand and shook Alexander's shoulder, and Alexander tried to shrug him off, before snapping awake.

"Wardrobe," Miles said simply. Alexander stretched in his seat like a cat, and stood. He seemed to sway a little for a couple of seconds, before shaking his head and looking down at Miles, who was still sitting, watching.

"They want you, too?" Alexander asked.

"Yeah," Miles said, and plastered on a smile, standing. "Lead the way."

"I can't quite remember which one it was," Alexander admitted, and looked confused. Miles' stomach flipped. He didn't like this.

"I know the way," he said, and walked out of the trailer, checking over his shoulder to make sure Alexander was following.

Instead of heading to wardrobe, Miles rounded the back of the makeup trailer and stood still, causing Alexander to bump into him, which did nothing to quell Miles' fears.

"What did you take?" He asked, turning to face Alexander. "You don't have allergies, do you? Please, my dad's a cop. What did you take?"

Alexander shook his head.

"Can we not?" He said, voice small, and Miles wished they couldn't, but he was *scared.*

"I'm worried about you. What did you take?" Miles repeated. Alexander reached into his jacket, and pulled out a prescription packet. He handed it over to Miles wordlessly, looking for all the world like he'd rather be anywhere else, shrinking inwards on himself, his fingers slipping away from Miles' as soon as they touched.

Valium. A dose that seemed too high. And Alexander had taken two of them.

"People touching me. I don't – it helps. If I can be – numb. It's like I'm floating a bit above everything. I don't like people in my space. They're going to – it's my job. I know it's my job. But I don't have to like it." Alexander spat out the last sentence.

"You could have told me," Miles said. "I could have – done something. You didn't have to do this."

"I don't want people knowing. It's not for much longer, right? Five years, at best. They'll get sick of me. In the meantime, I cope. I'm doing this because I want to, Miles, for you."

Miles flipped over the packet, looking at all the warnings. The side effects.

"How long have you been on these?" Miles asked, dreading the answer.

Alexander shook his head again, as if trying to clear it and run away from the answer at the same time.

"Sixteen years," he said. "That sounds about right."

"Alexander, that's half your life," Miles said, horrified.

Alexander smiled, and it looked ugly. Wrong. All teeth but in the worst way.

"I know. And I know it's fucking up my liver, too. But I can't work if I don't take them. I can't go out if I don't take them. I don't feel *safe*. Do you know what that's like? Not to feel safe?"

"Alexander – " Miles started, and had a flash of sitting with Jacob in that blanket fort after the death threat. Another flash, of holding his mother's cold hand and listening to the machine beside her drone, knowing even as a kid what that meant. "Alexander, I could have done something."

"Please just let me do my job. That's all you can do," Alexander said, sounding tired. His eyes looked a little brighter though, as though the worst of the fog had cleared. "I've been doing this a long time."

Too long, Miles thought but didn't say.

"Please just tell me if you feel any of these," Miles pointed at the side effects list. "Don't just – this is just a music video. It's not real."

"I'll be fine. Scout's honour," Alexander said, and his smile was hollow. "You won't even know. Nobody ever does."

"You know how scary that sounds?" Miles asked, despite himself.

"I am vaguely self-aware, so yes, actually. But I'm also a professional." Alexander snapped back.

"This – this isn't professional," Miles said, sadness and confusion turning to anger.

"Half the people here are on something. It's five thirty in the fucking morning and they're running around with their asses on fire. You think that's normal?" Alexander snarled, and Miles took a step back. Alexander sighed, and leaned back against the trailer. "I'm sorry. You're right. It's fucked up. I'm fucked up. I forget how much sometimes until somebody points it out to me, and then I don't tend to take it very well."

"Is it only at work?" Miles asked, thinking back to every text, every phone call. Had he ever met a Alexander who wasn't shrouded behind sedation?

"I was on them the night I met you, if that's what you're asking. But not at home. Only when I have to work or go out. I'm not – I mean, I need them, but I'm not addicted. Just when people could – when people are around."

"Fuck," Miles breathed.

"We need to get to wardrobe," Alexander reminded him, and Miles knew he was closing the subject down. "We'll talk, after. I owe you that."

"You don't owe me anything, Alexander," Miles promised, meaning every word. His heart ached in his chest as Alexander closed his eyes for a few seconds, clenching his jaw.

"Everyone says that. They never mean it."

"I mean it," Miles said softly.

Alexander opened his eyes, and looked right at Miles, as though he was looking right through him. Miles felt oddly exposed.

"Maybe you do," Alexander said, and pushed himself up from the trailer he was leaning against. He started heading towards wardrobe. Miles followed, thoughts already scattering in a million directions, creating, and then trying to solve, a problem.

*

The worst thing was, Alexander was right. If Miles hadn't seen the initial hit, he'd never have noticed Alexander was on something. Alexander was personable and kind to the people in wardrobe, and once they were dressed, he continued to act entirely professional as he was given his cues.

Americana blasted over hidden speakers, cutting off over and over as they got the takes they needed. Miles thought he might be going insane, in a version of Groundhog Day where his friend - and he could say that, Alexander *was* his friend, *his* friend - had to sedate himself to cope. And people were manhandling him into place, like they didn't know that. And they didn't know. Nobody knew, only Miles.

He must have opened his mouth a dozen times to tell someone to get their hands off Alexander's body, before closing it again. It wouldn't help Alexander, not in the short term or the long run. He just had to grit his teeth and get through it.

Alexander was doing this for him.

Fuck.

But Alexander had a career. Alexander did this a lot. Did that make it better or worse? Did Jacob know? Miles supposed he had to, because Jacob was good at knowing about this kind of thing.

Miles was getting a headache.

He'd hugged Alexander. Alexander hadn't seemed to hate it. Was that acting, too? Or had Alexander taken more Valium before he'd even got here? Did he need it even for Miles? Why did that hurt? Miles wasn't entitled to special treatment. They'd known each other for a couple of weeks. Sure, it felt longer, but –

Miles was chasing himself in circles. He tried and failed to mouth along to the lyrics of the song, looking into the camera and pretending he actually cared if this video turned out to be a shitshow or not. Alexander was standing behind the camera, just off to one side, and he looked every inch the classic American bad boy, leather jacket hanging off his frame like it'd been hand sewn for him. Miles hated the way his heart still flipped when he looked at him, because he couldn't let himself be one of those people who wanted to touch Alexander, who wanted to use him.

He thought back to the bar, and his first impression of Alexander, and how Alexander had seemed boring. Just another semi-famous face in the crowd. Attractive, but in a very bland way.

Compare and contrast to how Miles felt now, how Miles had learnt the curves of Alexander's face, jutting cheekbones and the strong brow that should make him terrifying or ugly but didn't. The stubble that was always perfect, in the way only money could make it. Miles couldn't deny he'd looked at Alexander's body, he knew the kind of perfection Alexander was hiding away, even if he hadn't Googled him to confirm it.

God, he felt sick. He stuttered over a line and apologised to the camera person, wincing as they wound the music back again. He was starting to hate this song.

He felt Alexander's eyes on him even when Miles wasn't looking at him. The medication seemed to drop Alexander's guard a little, and Miles thought back to that brush of knuckles and the nausea rose again, because he'd held that as something precious when really Alexander – was he even in control of his actions? He had to be vulnerable, in some way, because nobody could function with that much Valium in them. And yet – Miles flicked a quick glance behind the camera, Alexander *looked* fine.

They were going to talk. Miles had that to hold onto. Except, he was worried about what exactly Alexander had to tell him. Sixteen years, and Alexander was thirty two. The math there was – it was bad. More puzzle pieces were dropping into place and Miles didn't like the picture they were making.

Miles made it to the end of the song for what must have been to the hundredth time, and the camera wasn't reset for another take. The light was fading, and bugs were buzzing into the bulbs set up to light him.

"If we could get the bathtub scene done, we can probably call it," the director said, and Miles knew there was a reason he hated him. Miles and Alexander had both taken turns being draped artistically across farm machinery, as predicted, and there had been a lot of moody shots of them looking off at the horizon, separately, together, mix and match. The bathtub hadn't come up, and Miles had kind of hoped it was a rejected idea.

Miles walked around the camera to Alexander, who seemed calm and at ease. Miles guessed he kind of had to be, though he hadn't seen him take any more pills since that morning. He wasn't sure how long they lasted, but it couldn't be all day, could it? So either Alexander was sneakier than Miles gave him credit for, or they had to be wearing off. At least the bathtub scene was the last one and they were done. Wrapped in a day, could be worse.

"We want both of you for this," someone - a woman, Miles wasn't sure what her job was - said to them, or at them, at least.

"Tell me you have hot water," Alexander said, and his smile seemed a little frayed at the edges.

"I think so, I don't know, it's not my job," the woman said, and looked a little harassed. It had been a long day, for everybody. She'd probably been here longer than Miles had. Tensions were going to start rising soon as everyone crossed over the fourteen hour day threshold.

"You think they'll want us to bathe together?" Alexander asked Miles quietly, following the woman out of the barn, kicking up hay as he went. "That wasn't – they didn't mention that."

"Is it going to be a problem?" Miles asked, and hated how it came out, like Alexander was demanding too much. "I mean, I can ask them to cut it."

"It's fine," Alexander said, but Miles could see the way the muscle in his jaw was jumping as he grit his teeth.

"If you need to stop – " Miles offered, but was cut off by Alexander.

"It's fine," he repeated.

Miles held his hands up in surrender.

"It's been a long day, I feel like shit, let's just get this done, yeah?" Alexander said, and Miles wanted to pat his arm or something, some kind of reassurance. He offered a small smile instead.

"We don't have to get dinner after," Miles said, remembering Alexander's promise.

"We've got a lot to talk about," Alexander replied, and Miles shook his head.

"We don't have to do it today," Miles said, because they didn't. It'd been a long day. Alexander was looking more tired by the minute. They could just be done.

"I need to tell you, Miles. You deserve to know. I can't – it's the kind of thing I can't not tell you.

Not if we're going to be – " he searched for the right word, "friends." It didn't sound like the word he wanted to say, but Miles didn't call him out on it.

Miles could recognise messy when he saw it, and this was it, again, wasn't it? And he couldn't resent Alexander for that, but he was so tired.

"Okay," he said. "Let's go get wet."

Chapter Five

"Our heartbeats make an anthem

They beat against the drum against the sky

I'm forged steel and you're panned gold

We're the promised destiny

They love us, they love us

Until they don't anymore

Thrift store rejects

Idols on sale for fifty cents."

- Americana, Miles Montgomery

*

@Montgomeryupdates: *Alexander Raine spotted playing Miles' love interest for #americana music video!*

*

The director walked around the bathtub, sizing both Alexander and Miles up, like dolls he was about to play with rather than human beings, taking in every inch of them. He nodded to himself. Miles felt suddenly nervous.

People were pouring water in now, and it had to be lukewarm at best, given the lack of steam rising from it in the increasingly cold night air.

"I want him," the director pointed at Miles, "lying back in the bath, clothes on, soaked to the bone. And I want him," now the director gestured to Alexander, "can we swing for his ass to be out? I think it'd make the scene. Put him on top of Montgomery, America's innocence lost, give the right-wing something to really complain about."

Miles could feel Alexander tense beside him.

"That wasn't in the – they didn't mention nudity," Alexander said, almost too quiet for the director to hear.

"Son, I've read your contract, as far as I can tell I can do what I like with you. I could have you bare ass, full frontal if I wanted, so don't test me," the director gritted out, calm belying a tired anger.

"No," Miles said, before Alexander could reply. "I don't like it."

"Sweetheart, I don't care what you *like*," the director turned on him, "you're America's *dream boy*, being corrupted by something everybody wants but few get to have. You want to trend on Twitter, don't you? Want to make a big deal? You're suddenly precious now?" He looked between Miles and Alexander, and saw the way Miles had unconsciously edged closer to Alexander. The director scoffed. "Oh, sweetheart, tell me you don't care about this piece of meat."

Alexander shuddered, and Miles couldn't even bear to look at him because he knew he'd lose it, his temper, his ability to remain calm at all.

"He's not a piece of meat, don't – you don't get to call him that. And I'm not your sweetheart. I'm veto-ing this. You don't get to do this to him."

The director cocked his head. "He's done worse, haven't you, Raine?"

Alexander let out something that could have been a whimper, and Miles snapped, because this wasn't *fair*. None of it was fair. Miles shouldn't have to be here. Alexander was only here to do Miles a favour. None of it was worth this. His masters weren't worth destroying someone over, and Miles looked at Alexander and knew he was putting all his effort into not falling apart.

"Using someone's history against them is a fucking lowball," Miles said, voice all steel now. "And what Alexander may or may not have consented to in the past has no bearing on what he feels comfortable doing today." Miles breathed out through his nose, harsh. "You know what?" He stepped away from Alexander, and pulled his own shirt over his head, knocking the cross necklace someone had put on him at some point during the day. He wasn't even fucking religious. It was all pretence. He was done.

He shucked his pants next, leaving him standing in his boxers. He hated being naked in front of people, but goddamn, he was throwing himself in front of a bullet here.

"You want a performance? Use me. And I mean that in the most literal sense. *Use* me. My ass. My dick, if you want it. Alexander stays clothed. Put him on the side of the bath. Have him pouring water over me. Make it a redemption. A blessing. Find some way to spin it that sounds pretentious enough to work. I don't care. I am so fucking over this shit. I will walk. I will post on every social media account I have telling people not to buy this single. I will ruin your name in the press. Yeah, you know I have that power. People hate me, but they believe me."

Miles bent and pulled his boxers down, standing naked and shivering, before hooking a leg over the side of the bathtub. His foot hit the cold water and he suppressed a shiver. He submerged himself, skin breaking out into goosebumps. He looked at the director straight in the eye, and then at Alexander, whose face was open and awed and a thousand other words that Miles would love to explore if he wasn't sitting naked in a cold bath in front of a couple dozen people.

"Are we doing this?" Miles asked, and it was a challenge.

The director huffed, and grunted. "You're a psychopath," he said to Miles, before turning to Alexander. "I'm going to make sure you never work again."

What little colour there was in Alexander face drained out, but he bit his lip and said nothing.

"Somebody get a fucking mug, we're going with this asshole's idea!" The director shouted, and stormed off.

Alexander leant down to the side of the bath, and Miles resisted the urge to cover himself with his hands. It felt like it'd be worse somehow, like admitting how bad this felt.

"You didn't have to do that," Alexander said softly.

"Yeah, I really did," Miles disagreed. "He had no right to talk to you like that."

"So what, you just – step into the line of fire instead?" Alexander asked, and seemed genuinely bewildered.

"What he said. Between the bluster, I listened. And what you've told me, well I've listened to that too. I dragged you into this. I don't want you to have to do something you regret."

"I'm already damaged goods," Alexander said, voice barely there. "You don't have to be, too."

"You're shaking," Miles said, and pressed a wet finger to Alexander's jacketed forearm.

"So are you," Alexander pointed out.

"I'm really fucking naked right now and at least five people have taken pictures and think I haven't noticed. I'm really trying hard not to think about that. God, this is – I never would have asked you. Not if I'd've known."

"It's okay," Alexander said. "We're nearly done, right? We're nearly done." He leaned in closer. "I'm going to steal this jacket."

Miles barked out a laugh.

"You're amazing," he said, and Alexander shrugged.

"You are," he said simply, in response.

The director was rampaging back towards them, a chipped hand thrown mug dangling from his fingers.

"Absolution, washing clean of sins, fucking religious symbolism, I don't care, I'm not getting paid enough for this. Raine, sit your ass on the side of the bath and put your feet in, boots and all. Contrast. Pour the water over his face. Like you love him," the director scoffed. "Montgomery, just act like the slut that you are. Shouldn't be too outside of your comfort zone."

"Don't," Miles muttered to Alexander, as the other man puffed up to defend him. "It's easier if you don't."

"Just focus on me," Alexander murmured back, as he got into position, scooting his booted feet beneath Miles' thighs. There was something grounding about that. "I'll make sure it doesn't get in your eyes."

The director thrust the mug at Alexander and the lights came on, and all Miles could see were the bulbs and the bugs before Alexander made a small noise in the back of his throat and brought Miles back to him. "Miles," he said gently. The way only he could.

In the end, it was as easy as it could be, given everything. Miles knew it'd look amazing, that it'd trend, that he'd won the power play. In an otherwise mediocre video, this was the scene people would remember. And none of that mattered. What mattered were the soft reminders from Alexander to close his eyes, to the way Alexander rested a hand on Miles' shoulder and massaged the bone there, working the shivers out of him. The world narrowed down to just the two of them, and Miles forgot about being naked, forgot about the cameras, forgot about *Americana* playing on a loop in the background.

When they were done, nobody moved at first to hand Miles a towel, so Alexander swung his feet out of the bath to do it himself, holding out a hand to help Miles up, using his body to shield Miles' own. He wrapped the towel around Miles' shoulders and stared at him for a long minute before pulling him close, rubbing his hands up and down Miles' arms to warm him.

Miles didn't realise he was crying at first, not until the first sob escaped.

"Thank you," Alexander whispered, broken.

The truth is, Miles would have done it a thousand times. It hadn't even been a choice he'd had to make.

Alexander's fingers wrapped around Miles' for the shortest couple of seconds, squeezing before letting go.

"Thank you," he repeated, and stepped back.

*

@BUZZFEED: *Miles Montgomery bares all in new video, dating Alexander Raine buzzfeed.com/Miles-mont…*

*

TRENDING

#MilesMontgomery

#americana

#AlexanderRaine

#Milesuncut

#Milesnudes

#malex

*

They headed back to Brooklyn together in the same car, and when Miles had looked at him, by unspoken agreement, Alexander had rattled off his address. He'd been right, it wasn't as fancy as Miles', but god, that really didn't matter right now. Miles just needed to sit somewhere comfortable and not think about anything for a long time.

He knew Alexander wanted to talk. *Needed* to talk, from the way he kept shooting glances at Miles and opening his mouth to start a sentence before closing it again, thinking better. Miles had to turn away, to look at the city lights bursting past, sparking up the night.

At some point, Alexander had hooked his little finger through Miles', bridging the gap between them even though they were sitting as far apart as they could in the back of the car. Miles was too tired to try to figure out what that meant, except, there was some part of him that knew they were never, ever going to be *just friends*.

And that scared him. Not for himself, because he didn't know how to be scared for himself anymore, but for Alexander. Alexander who he knew he could write about endlessly. Alexander who was shaped exactly like somebody Miles could love.

This night promised nothing good, except maybe the beginning of catharsis. A confession, hastily spilled, perhaps.

Miles couldn't hope for any more than that, and tried to ease the feeling of want in his belly. It wasn't sex, it wasn't as base as that. God, that'd be easier. It was the kind of want that stretched into the months and years ahead, a want that wanted a future.

Miles didn't know if he could give Alexander a future, or if Alexander even wanted one with him.

And yet, Miles' head turned the same thoughts over and over, watching the cars pass them, feeling the warmth of Alexander's pinky wrapped around his.

Alexander was wearing the leather jacket. He'd walked out with it, just like he'd promised Miles he would. It looked good on him, blacker than black in the dark of the car. Miles wondered if taking a memento of such a bad day was a way of coping. He thought he might prefer to forget, given the option. But at the same time –

There was something to be said for sharing the same scars. Miles had screamed it in his every action, *show me yours and I'll show you mine*. And Alexander hadn't even flinched. Everybody flinched away from Miles Montgomery.

But Alexander only saw *Miles*.

Miles had turned his phone off that morning, and though he could see Alexander moving his own through the fingers of his spare hand, the screen never lit up. Miles wondered if he'd ever turn his phone on again, after today. There was a clarity to what he'd done now that hadn't been there at the time. He'd been naked in every possible sense, not a tasteful artist's nude, but naked in the barest, most warts and all way. There had to be photos. He knew there were. Not just of Miles himself, but of Alexander helping him back into his clothes, the intimacy that carried. The way they'd moved as one to leave, the undeniable way they had merged into one being, in some irreversible way.

Alexander had seen him cry. And he'd seen Alexander sedate, sedated, malleable.

He would have walked away from his masters for Alexander. That threat had been in the air. The weight of it hit him. *He could have lost his music.* What the fuck. He would have given up everything for this man. He was doing it again, wasn't he? God, he hoped it was worth it. It felt like it was. He shivered a little, and he could feel Alexander's eyes on him again.

"Cold?" Alexander asked. Miles shook his head.

"Tired," he said, because that just about summed it up.

"I'm sorry," Alexander said, the same tiredness reflected in his features.

"It's not your fault," Miles replied, and he could hear the rustle of leather as Alexander shook his head.

"Doesn't mean I don't get to be sorry."

The first night, Alexander had said nobody had ever apologised before. For what happened to him. For what he was going to tell Miles had happened to him.

The weight of Alexander's apology meant something. It settled deep into Miles' bones.

He looked over at Alexander, and just allowed himself to look. And Alexander allowed it, too.

"It was a really long day," Miles said.

"Yeah," Alexander replied, and sighed a little. "Feel like it's not over yet."

"We don't have to do this tonight," Miles said, and moved his little finger to hold Alexander's a little tighter. It was such a small motion, but it felt like everything.

"If I don't tell you tonight – Miles, I'm going to let you walk away. If I don't tell you, that's what's going to happen. This isn't an act of bravery on my part, it's an act of cowardice. Because however much it's going to hurt to tell you, it'd hurt more to watch you leave."

It wasn't a game of cheques and balances with them, it never had been. The scales had always been level. And yet, Alexander still felt like he owed Miles something.

"I'm not going to leave. I don't think I ever could have. You didn't want messy. And I'm sorry. Because I look at you and all I can think about is all the ways I could ruin your life by caring about you," Miles said, honest, letting the words hang in the air.

"That's a hell of a thing to believe about yourself," Alexander said, quietly. Looking at Miles, as Miles looked at him. Seeing Miles, in a way that made Miles more exposed than New Jersey, more than anything. He somehow managed to hold eye contact, but it was a close thing.

"It's true, though," Miles said tentatively.

"I think you believe it, but I don't think that makes it true."

"What's the difference?" Miles asked.

"Intent, I think. What you plan on doing with that knowledge," Alexander said, like it was easy.

"I know I'd leave before I let anyone hurt you. Myself included," Miles said.

"That doesn't sound like you're planning on ruining my life," Alexander pointed out.

"Alexander, you don't date. We can't – be *anything*."

Alexander growled, and Miles startled a little.

"I'm sorry," Alexander said, "it's just. I'm so tired of myself. Of being the way I am. Of the constant fucking hyper vigilance. Not deserving. Never deserving. It's exhausting."

"You're allowed to want things," Miles said carefully. "And they can be entirely on your terms. I'm never going to push you to do – god, anything. I think I'd die before I tried."

"I don't know how to do any of this," Alexander said. "I never have. I don't think I'm going to be any good at it."

The car rolled to a gentle stop outside an apartment block. Alexander unhooked his finger from Miles', but didn't move beyond that.

"Let's just talk for a while," Miles said into the quiet.

Alexander nodded.

They got out of the car, and Alexander keyed in the code for the front door.

Miles followed him over the threshold, and found he was holding his breath. He let it out, slow and steady.

They were going to talk.

Chapter Six

When Miles stepped into Alexander's apartment, he was a little surprised. It was smaller than he'd expected, probably the smallest in the block of apartments, though by Brooklyn standards it was reasonable, if unexpected for someone who had money like Alexander did.

What took Miles aback was the lack of *stuff*. Spartan was one way to describe it, unlived in could be another. There were a few shelves on the wall, but they didn't seem deliberate, Miles could imagine Alexander inherited them when he bought the place rather than putting them up himself. They carried a few objects, a couple of framed photos and a small stack of books, but nothing that screamed Alexander's personality at Miles.

It was just an apartment. It was a place to live. Like Alexander was waiting for it not to be anymore.

"It's nice," he said, for wont of anything else to say, and he heard Alexander scoff behind him, and the rustle of Alexander removing the leather jacket.

"It's empty, I know. Jacob has had words about it. I need to put down some roots, right? I just – I like being able to look at all my stuff and know if I had to leave in a hurry I could. There's nothing holding me here, I could just go," Alexander explained, and moved through to the small kitchen, opening the fridge. "Do you want a drink?"

"Just water, please," Miles said, and watched as Alexander took down two of three glasses from a cupboard and poured some water from a filter. He noticed Alexander's hands were shaking, as the water slopped lazily onto the counter top.

"Hey, Alexander," Miles said gently, and moved to take the glass from him before he dropped it. "It's okay. Not leaving, remember? Unless you want me to. We don't – we still don't have to do this."

"The director knew," Alexander said. "That means it's out there. In the world. She's let it get out. She's fucking swinging the blade closer and closer to my neck. You need to know what you're getting into."

Alexander grunted and gave up on pouring his own water, the glass half empty as he set it on the side and moved to wipe up the mess. Miles wanted to reach out to still him, but instead could only watch Alexander's jerky movements as he robotically wiped the counter down and put the filter back in the fridge.

"Do you need to take something? Would that help?" Miles said, hating that he had to say it, but knowing now that the medication had to have worn off hours ago and Alexander hadn't taken more, had probably been on edge since long before the bathtub scene. God, Miles just wanted to hug him, but he didn't think he should.

Alexander shook his head.

"After, maybe. I need to be present for this. I need to make sure you – know. All of it. Or as much as I can tell. It's like. There's a taboo on what I can say. Like my tongue stops working. But I'm going to try for you, Miles."

Miles took a sip of his water, and watched Alexander try to decide where to sit, on the couch or the small armchair. They'd either be beside each other or facing each other at an angle, the armchair offered more separation, but not by much.

Alexander chose the armchair. Miles settled on the couch, deliberately sitting in the middle, so he could move closer or further away if Alexander needed it.

Alexander tried to drink, but choked on his first sip, and had to clear his throat. He put his glass down on the cheap IKEA coffee table and red-faced, rubbed a hand over his eyes. He looked at Miles, then away, staring at an empty patch of wall.

"I was fifteen," he started.

Miles' stomach dropped.

"I was fifteen," Alexander repeated, "and it was my first big job. A teen magazine wanted me for a photo shoot. They were going to fly me out to New York. I'd never been before, we grew up in Ohio. It was exciting, you know? I'd been asked for specially, by the photographer. She'd – she'd asked for me specifically.

"And I felt special. I felt like this was the beginning of everything, that this would make me famous. You know, when you're a kid, you think everything's going to be the catalyst to your life changing. So, I met – her. Samantha. Dammit, I should be able to say her name."

Alexander looked down at his hands for a long moment. Miles almost opened his mouth to speak before Alexander spoke again.

"Samantha Sink."

Miles stilled.

"Sink?" He asked carefully, not wanting to interrupt Alexander, but needing to know.

It wasn't a common surname.

Alexander looked at him, then back to the space on the wall.

"Have you heard of her?" He asked, voice very small, wary.

Miles shook his head.

"No, just – wondered if I'd heard right," he said.

"Okay," Alexander said, and blew out a breath. "She had this – set. A bedroom. Like, a teenage boy's bedroom. God, it even looked like mine. She had it perfect to the smallest detail. I could have lived there, you know? It was my life reflected back at me. I thought she must know me so well. As though every bedroom in the country didn't look exactly the same. I was stupid. Naïve.

"She – she wasn't stupid. Or naïve. She saw how excited I was. How willing I was to please. We took some photos. For the magazine. It was fun, dressing up in clothes I didn't think I'd ever be able to afford. I – I asked if I could keep them. As a joke. She said yes. That they looked so good on me that she insisted. Then she – said she bet I looked even better out of them."

Miles' heart hammered in his chest and he could already see where this was heading, and it felt like being tied to the railway tracks, with the train closing in, he could almost hear the bellow of the horn, the puff of the engines, the digging in of the rails into his spine bones. He ached for Alexander; for fifteen year old Alexander, for Alexander now, Alexander whose breathing had gone raggedy and harsh.

"Is it weird that she seems young to me now? The day I realised I'd turned older than she was when she'd – when it'd happened, I was twenty six. She was twenty six when she – when she took those photos. I was fifteen. And I *smiled* for them."

Alexander spat his words out. Like he'd done something wrong. As though he hadn't been preyed upon.

"She has everything. She wanted to take everything from me. I was a virgin and she loved that. Told me it was delicious. I was in that bedroom that could have been my bedroom and I didn't know how to say no. So I didn't. I sort of – let it happen. I lay there and let it happen. And I knew, abstractly, that one of the cameras was recording us. It was – it felt grownup. That she wanted photos of me doing that stuff and she wanted it recorded. It was scary, I mean, I'd been on the internet and even back then I knew how things could spread, but she promised me, god, she promised me it'd be our secret. That she loved me enough that she just wanted me for herself."

Alexander stopped, and Miles watched his shoulders begin to shake, watched as he started to fall apart.

"That's enough now," Miles said. "You can stop."

Alexander sniffed roughly and shook his head.

"I left New York after three days. She took so many photos. My hand on my dick – my – stuff I – I can't talk about. She liked toys. Liked them in me. I didn't like that, but she said I made the prettiest faces. I wanted to be a model, Miles, and she was telling me I was pretty. She knew exactly which buttons to push.

"I have to believe I was the only one. I know that's not going to be the truth of it, but it's been seventeen years and I've never said a word against her. What if other people have gotten hurt because of me? What if I could have stopped her? Fuck, my parents were so proud, they still have copies of the magazine. I – the clothes. When I got home I couldn't even look at them. They smelt like her. Smelt like all the things she'd made me do. It didn't sink in all at once. I was so young, I didn't understand. At first I just knew it was wrong. That she'd done something wrong. It took me a long time to realise that it was a power thing. It was all about power. Every day I wait for those photos to show up somewhere. She could leak them at any time. It's me. It's obviously me. My face – it's in enough of them. I was so fucking stupid. So fucking young."

"Fuck, Alexander," Miles breathed, and he didn't know what to do. Didn't know what to say. "Alexander, you were a *kid*. It wasn't your fault."

"I know," Alexander said roughly, "but who's going to believe me? When it finally comes out, and it will, who the fuck is going to believe me?"

He was shaking so violently Miles was worried he was going to have a seizure or something.

"Alexander, please, drink some water," he said, and Alexander seemed to remember that Miles was there, his fingers clenching and unclenching on the glass as his eyes flicked to Miles' and away again. He obeyed, like a puppet, taking small sips whilst Miles tried to figure out how to navigate this.

"I feel like if I tell someone, all they can see is her. Like she marked me. Like all I am is an extension of her. I was right, that those photos would make me famous. I don't know how much she had to do with that, whether I owe everything to her. Maybe I do. Maybe she made sure my body would, *could* only ever be a commodity. I – I thought I could get over it. I've tried to have sex with other people. Since. But the second they touch me I want to die. And I'm scared I won't be able to say no. I'm fucked up about consent. I understand that. So I don't. I don't date. I don't fuck. I don't pass on the stain of her to anybody else," Alexander paused, looking at Miles now, face a wreck of emotions, eyes red and swollen, and Miles had thought catharsis could be beautiful but he'd been wrong.

"Jacob talks about you a lot," Alexander continued. "He told me you're good. That you don't hurt people. He told me about the blanket fort, about the bat. How you stayed with him that night even though he'd said terrible things about you to the press. I wanted to meet you. I'd mentioned it, in passing. Because what people were saying about you and what Jacob was saying didn't match up. And so there you were, at the bar, drinking orange juice, and he told me to go talk to you. He – he thinks, I mean, I've told him. About her. But he doesn't understand it. He thinks it's just something I have to get over."

Alexander paused to raise a hand as though he knew Miles wanted to argue, to protest. He sighed heavily before continuing.

"He has his shit too, right? And he's fine. But I don't know if I can believe that, I don't know if I'll ever be clean of her. Not whilst I know she still has those photos. The video. She'd ruin herself to ruin me, you know? So I've kept my head down. But seeing you at the bar. The things Jacob had said about you. I almost believed – no, for the first time, I actually believed I could be a normal human being. I saw you, and I *wanted*. And that terrified me. You have no idea, when you asked if you could get in the car with me, how close I came to saying yes."

"Then I'm glad you said no," Miles said. "God, Alexander. I'm so sorry. I'm so, so sorry that happened to you."

"If I'm seen with you, if you're seen with me, she could – I've always been hers, haven't I? And if you take me away from her, she'll do something. And I really like you, Miles. I didn't even know I could anymore. But I do. I know you would never hurt me."

"You can't know that," Miles said.

Alexander shook his head.

"That's exactly how I know. Because you just said that. She would convince me I was right. That I was safe. They wouldn't point out the danger. You don't realise how singular you are. Miles Montgomery: Not the icon, but the man. I'm not scared of you, because I don't think you would hurt me. Because you never would. I'm scared of being with you because of her. Because I could tarnish you. And I'm scared that I'm willing to risk it. What you did for me today, what you kept doing for me today, from the pills to the bathtub, even the way you looked like you were going to start a fight every time somebody touched me."

Miles thought back earlier to the video shoot, to the fierce protective urge he'd felt. He'd probably tear the world apart for this man, if Alexander only said the word.

"I'm selfish," Alexander continued, "and I want you in my life. I don't know what to do. I don't know what to do, Miles. You hugged me this morning and it felt safe. I wanted it. Do you know how long it's been since somebody touched me and I haven't felt my skin crawling?"

Alexander looked wrecked, in the worst way. Miles couldn't imagine he looked any better himself. There was so much Miles could say to Alexander, about how nothing Samantha had done could ever hurt Miles the way Alexander believed it would. But that could come later. Now, Alexander needed comfort, what little Miles could provide.

"Alexander, can I touch your hand?" He asked, and waited carefully for Alexander to nod. He shuffled closer to the armchair, telegraphing his movements in an exaggerated manner. He reached out, slowly, and placed his hand over

Alexander's, wrapping his fingers around Alexander's fingers, holding on, awkward, but there.

They sat like that for a long time, Miles holding on, Alexander letting him hold on. There weren't words, none that would fix this. But when Alexander moved his hand under Miles', facing his palm up so their fingers slotted together, curling his fingers between the cracks of Miles' own, it didn't feel hopeless. And Miles could see that in Alexander's eyes too, in the tiny impossible smile trying to break through, like sunshine behind a cloud.

How did it go, again?

Hope is the thing with feathers.

*

Alexander yawned, and raised a hand to try stifle it. They'd been sitting for a long time, and Miles' muscles ached with it. Outside the window, it wasn't so dark anymore.

"Do you want me to leave? So you can sleep?" Miles asked.

Alexander shook his head. "I don't think I could sleep. Not now. But at the same time, I'm so tired. I feel like I've had flu for a week. Like I need to sleep but my body won't let me."

Miles tugged gently on Alexander's hand, where their fingers were still interlaced.

"Tell me, at any point, no matter how stupid it might feel. Tell me and I'll stop. You trust me, right? Then trust me when I say I'll stop. I'm going to scoot over to the end of the couch, and I'll grab some cushions, and you can put your head in my lap, or on my thigh. And I'll keep watch while you sleep. How does that sound?" Miles asked, watching Alexander's reaction carefully, the slow acceptance crossing his face.

"I won't sleep," Alexander said slowly, around another yawn, "but we could try it."

"Resting is better than nothing," Miles said. "My dad used to tell me that. When my brain was spiralling about a million things at once, he'd tell me to go lie down, because it was still rest. It still counted."

Alexander moved slowly, sleep-stumbling his way over to the couch, not letting go of Miles' hand. Miles used his other hand to gather up some cushions and he made a nest of them for Alexander's head, scooting across the couch as much as he could so that Alexander could lie down fully.

Alexander paused for a moment, and Miles looked up at him to check in, but Alexander nodded, that small smile still there, and everything felt so close to shattering, but somehow bulletproof all at once.

"I'm okay, Miles. Just figuring out how not to squash you."

"I'll be fine," Miles promised. Even if he got no sleep tonight, and it didn't look like he would, he'd be fine. He'd walk through fire for Alexander. He knew that now.

Alexander settled himself on the couch, and looked up at Miles for a long moment before turning his face into Miles' stomach. Maybe that felt safer. Miles wasn't going to judge. He pulled down a blanket from the back of the couch and carefully placed it over Alexander's prone form.

"Can you stroke my hair?" Alexander asked, muffled. "When I was a kid, before everything, my mom used to stroke my hair after a bad dream. It helped. Maybe it'll help now, too."

Miles placed his hand slowly into the muss of Alexander's hair, still full of product, and let it rest for a moment before moving his fingers. Alexander sighed with it.

"I'm just going to close my eyes," he murmured. "I'm not sleeping, but I'm just going to close my eyes for a bit."

"Whatever you want, Alexander," Miles said. "I'm here. For as long as you need."

Alexander made a small noise in the back of his throat and pushed a little closer to Miles, and Miles kept moving his fingers through Alexander's hair, stroking down to the delicate patch of skin behind his ear, then back up again.

He couldn't pinpoint the exact moment Alexander fell asleep, only that his breathing evened out and his body went lax and heavy in a way it hadn't been before. Miles kept moving his fingers, staring at the bare room.

And then, with the sun turning the small room orange, his head tipped back and his eyes slipped closed, his hand resting against the swell of Alexander's cheekbone. Miles slept, drenched in the rays of a new day.

*

Miles woke up confused for a moment as to where he was, before remembering, the warm weight in his lap, Alexander, the night before, the day they'd lived through before that. It was like downloading a video on an old modem, it came to him in chunks, piece by violent piece, and yet, when he looked down, all he saw was the way Alexander's face was nestled into his stomach, the way Miles' hand had dropped to rest on Alexander's neck.

He looked at Alexander, really looked, at how open his face was in sleep, at the smudged remnants of yesterday's makeup, at the way Alexander's hand was fisted in the bottom of Miles' shirt.

There wasn't a clock on the wall, but it had to be mid-morning, if not later. Miles didn't remember falling asleep, but he must have slept for a while. Alexander, too. He was glad for that.

His neck didn't thank him for it, and he tried to shift into a more comfortable position. He rolled his shoulders as gently as he could. It was enough to make Alexander whine against Miles and try to snuggle his face in closer, before pulling away, eyes wide and looking up at Miles sideways, suddenly wide awake.

"Hi," Miles said softly, and made to move his hand from Alexander's neck, not wanting to touch more than Alexander could permit. Alexander made a small noise as he removed it, and seemed reluctant as he unfurled his grasp from Miles' shirt. "Sleep okay?"

"Surprisingly, yes. I feel like I was hit by a bus, but in a good way," Alexander said, and shifted onto his back so that he could look up at Miles. Miles worried briefly about whether Alexander could see up his nose, before realising it really didn't matter. Alexander had seen everything. Alexander still wanted him.

They needed to talk about that, they really did. What that meant.

Miles' stomach rumbled, and Alexander smirked, ear close enough to really hear it.

"Breakfast?" Alexander asked, and Miles nodded.

"If you don't mind. I can go, if you'd prefer."

"Stay," Alexander said, and Miles knew that he would. For as long as Alexander asked him to. He pushed Alexander's hair back from where it had fallen flat across his forehead in sleep, and Alexander scrunched his brow up at the touch.

"It's weird that you can do that without me freaking out," he said.

Alexander's voice was kind of rusty, and Miles understood. Alexander had talked a lot last night, for a long time. Miles wanted to offer him a honey drink, like after a concert, but he doubted Alexander would have it. He didn't wanted to leave the safe bubble they'd built to go get it, but maybe in time. Alexander seemed lighter for it now though, even with the question of what they were and what that meant still hanging in the air between them.

"I'm glad I don't freak you out," Miles said. "But let me know if I do, won't you?"

"I will," Alexander said. Miles chose to believe him. Alexander had said he had consent issues, and Miles knew he needed to respect that. But he also needed to respect that Alexander was a grown man who could make his own choices. And that meant Miles got to make choices too, but in such a way that he would do his best to not cross any boundaries. It would be like walking through a field dotted with landmines, he knew that already. This easy peace couldn't last. Alexander had been living with this for seventeen years, and he must have spent every single day of those seventeen years waiting for the other shoe to drop. To feel that powerless, for that length of time, Miles couldn't imagine it. It made his worries about his own life feel very small.

But Alexander wouldn't want that, that was something Miles could respect, too. It would never work between them if Miles treated Alexander like spun sugar. Whilst there was now a before and an after to their relationship, the Alexander who had texted Miles and talked to Miles and acted like a little shit hadn't gone away. He was the same person. Miles had just seen more of him now. Whatever Alexander thought, Samantha hadn't stained him, hadn't ruined him for anybody else. Certainly hadn't ruined him for Miles. That Alexander had been strong for so long, that made him powerful, and Miles wasn't sure if Alexander realised that.

Miles' stomach rumbled again, and Alexander laughed.

"I'm cooking you pancakes," he said, and rolled off the couch onto the floor, making it look graceful somehow. He stood, and stretched. "The bathroom's that door there, if you want to use it. How do you feel about chocolate chips?"

"I feel very good about chocolate chips, generally and specifically," Miles said, and smiled. Alexander smiled back. "I'm going to, ya know, bathroom, now," Miles said, and gestured at the door Alexander had pointed out.

He went to the bathroom, and squeaked toothpaste over his teeth on his finger, and then paused. He knew the name Sink. It couldn't be a coincidence. His dad was drinking buddies with Christopher Sink, a local hunter, and even he'd pointed out how uncommon the surname was, and that was coming from a Montgomery. It was worth flagging up. For Alexander's sake.

Miles' phone was in his pocket, so he pressed the power on, not unlocking it, because the notifications that did pop up were scary enough: Twitter, Instagram, a few dozen missed calls and messages. He ignored it all and hit the Emergency Call button, that he'd long since programmed to be his father's number.

His father answered quickly, and Miles spoke in a low voice.

"Dad, this isn't a personal call. I wish it was. Do you still hang out with Christopher Sink?"

His dad answered in the affirmative, questioning why he was asking. Miles didn't have time, Alexander would be wondering if he'd drowned in the sink.

"Does he have a sister? A cousin? Samantha, a photographer. Something, some kind of relation?" Miles asked quietly, desperately.

"Son, what is it?" His father asked, and Miles bit his tongue, keeping Alexander's secret, but needing to do *something*.

"Just, look into her, could you? Off the record, but the kind of shit you don't want to find on somebody. The worst kind of shit. The sick stuff. Don't ask me why. Just. Please," Miles was close to begging.

"Are you in trouble?" His dad asked, and Miles smiled sadly to himself.

"I'm safe," Miles reassured him. "Just heard some pretty ugly rumours."

"I heard some about you, too," his dad replied, and Miles could only guess.

"They're probably true, but don't worry about them, okay, Dad? It's all for a good reason. I swear. I have to go, but I love you."

"I love you too, kiddo," his dad said, and Miles ended the call, turned off his phone, and slid it back into his pocket. He looked in the mirror and ran a hand through his hair. His eyeliner from yesterday was smudgy and made his eyes look huge. He didn't have the patience to try wash it off though.

He stepped out of the bathroom and was hit by the smell of perfectly cooked pancakes.

"I may have to marry you," he said without thinking, and Alexander chuckled.

"Not what I was expecting to hear," he said. "Given everything."

"Don't do that," Miles said, not wanting to break the mood, but not wanting Alexander to put himself down over something he couldn't possibly control. "The way I feel about you hasn't changed. Except now I know you make amazing pancakes, so maybe I'm a little fonder. Just a smidge."

"I put myself down a lot, huh?" Alexander said, and tilted his head to the side a little like he was thinking about it. "I don't think I realise I'm doing it. Nobody's ever pointed it out to me before."

"Well, I'm pointing it out now. And I'm going to keep pointing it out until you stop doing it. Now, are you going to feed me pancakes until I explode or are you going to keep teasing me?"

Miles asked, and sat down at the table, stomach rumbling in earnest now.

"I'm trying to understand how I'm allowed this," Alexander said, and served a huge fluffy pancake onto Miles' plate. "It doesn't seem real."

"It's just pancakes," Miles said, though they both knew that wasn't true.

He took a bite and moaned despite himself.

"Oh my fucking god," he said, and looked at Alexander, who'd pinked up a little.

"It's just pancakes," Alexander echoed back.

"Fuck off," Miles said. "You're a pancake god and you know it. Now, eat breakfast with me. You're missing out."

"For the first time, it doesn't feel like I am," Alexander admitted, and knocked his ankle against Miles' under the table. Miles moved his foot so that it covered Alexander's, just a little. It was nice. That word again, *nice*.

Miles thought about it. Nice was a good word. It didn't make demands, wasn't more than it needed to be. It just *was*.

Just like this moment.

Chapter Seven

It couldn't last. It never did. A ringing sound echoed through the apartment and Alexander looked up, confused.

"You have a landline?" Miles asked, bemused.

"Apparently," Alexander replied, and got up to search for it.

The ringing cut off as he answered, and his brow creased as he looked at Miles.

"It's Jacob," he said. "He needs to talk to you. It's urgent."

Miles felt just as confused.

"How did he know I was here?" He asked, as Alexander handed the phone over, and Alexander shrugged, then gestured for him to answer Jacob.

"If you're going to give me shit for yesterday – " Miles started pre-emptively, but Jacob interrupted, violently.

"Do not look at your phone. I don't care what you're doing with Alexander right now, but do not look at your phone. Him neither. I need you to trust me on this," Jacob barked, accent shining through in a way it rarely did these days. He sounded angry.

"I know they took photos of me yesterday," Miles said and shrugged. He'd expected the fallout, he just didn't understand why Jacob had tracked him down to – be mad at him?

"It's not that," Jacob said. "You really don't know, do you?"

"Know what?" Miles asked, and the concern in his voice must have been picked up by Alexander, who folded himself closer into Miles' personal space, as though he was trying to hear Jacob's words. "Speaker phone?" Miles mouthed to Alexander, who shook his head.

Jacob let out a long sigh, and Miles could just picture him, running a hand through his stupid curls and pacing. He would always pace when he was on the phone. Walking grooves into the earth.

"Since the photos from *Americana* dropped, about – six hours later, an anonymous account has been tweeting nudes of you and Alexander every half hour, amping it up each time. Two hours ago they doxxed you, your Brooklyn address. Every time a photo gets taken down, another one goes up. It's you and Alexander, Miles. I know they're fake, most people with half a brain cell will know they're fake, but they're the kind of fake that is just convincing enough that it might be true, you know?" Jacob said, words tumbling out. "Alexander's told you, hasn't he? What's at stake for him? Well, I think we know who's doing this. What their endgame might be. They've put a timer on – fuck – they've put a timer on releasing Alexander's home address. They're going to release it in an hour. Sooner, if another photo gets flagged."

"What the fuck," Miles said, and felt his knees bend as he folded down to the floor, huddling in on himself. He was aware of Alexander helping to guide him down, of Alexander nudging his chin over Miles' shoulder and his hands around Miles' waist. "Why is she doing this? Are you sure it's her?"

Alexander stiffened behind Miles, and Miles knew what he must be thinking and shook his head minutely to try signal, *not that*, not yet anyway.

Jacob made an unhappy noise. "The metadata from the photos is all completely scrubbed, so nobody can prove anything. So I can only say it's circumstantial, at best. Someone got a ping from a server in South Africa, but that's as localised as we can get it. Look, you need to get out of that apartment. I had my security drive past yours and it's a shitshow. Alexander can't handle that. Alexander isn't built for this like we are, you know that."

"What do I do, Jacob? What do I do?" Miles was panicking, because if it was just him, he could handle this. He'd been doxxed before, and he'd made his choice with the *Americana* video shoot. It didn't give anybody a right to do this, but he knew what he was signing up for, what he'd always been signing up for. Alexander had never signed up for any of this in the same way, he'd just gotten trapped in it. Miles tapped a finger against Alexander's knee, and rubbed a circle on the knobble of bone, to try to calm – who? Himself? Alexander? Both, probably.

"Jennifer's set your plane up, you can just leave. And I mean this in a very real sense. You can just leave. You've talked about it for long enough. Just go, Miles. You don't owe them anything anymore. You and Alexander, you need to get out of this country," Jacob said.

"I can't – what the fuck, I can't just - I can't do that to him. Where would we even – Jacob. Jacob, please – "

"We've talked about my London apartment a dozen times. It's still there. Nobody knows about it. This isn't a decision you get to pick and choose over. I'll give you the address, write it down, don't put it on your phone. You still have your spare passport, right?"

"It's in a lockbox at the airport, yeah," Miles said, automatically.

"Good, that's good. Now, the key to my apartment is under the gnome, you remember the gnome right?" Jacob said, and Miles would have laughed under better circumstances. There'd been a fuck ugly gnome statue outside Jacob's front door that Miles had always threatened to kick, more out of curiosity than anything. It didn't look like it was made out of any material known to man, and Miles wanted to see what would happen.

"Miles!" Jacob interrupted his nostalgia. "Write my address down. And the code for the gate. Jennifer's arranged a driver to meet you at the airport, they'll have it too, but just in case."

Miles nudged Alexander and made a writing gesture with his hand. Alexander scrunched his eyebrows in confusion before unhooking his chin from Miles' shoulder and getting up, returning with a notepad and pen.

"Okay," Miles said, mind reeling, unable to take any of this in. Alexander sat cross legged in front of him, eyes darting over Miles' face, trying to read him.

Jacob read off his address, and the key code, then had Miles repeat it back to him.

"Tell Alexander I'm sorry," Jacob said. "I don't think I ever told him that before. And I'm sorry to you, too, Miles. This is – this isn't how I thought you'd get to escape it all."

"My dad – " Miles said. "You need to tell my dad - tell him – fuck tell him I'm okay - tell him where I'll be - tell him - fucking fuck - tell him to call Theo's dad, FBI, right? Not to be too proud - tell him to find her - to find it all. He'll know. He'll know, Jacob."

"I'll tell him," Jacob promised. "Theo? Okay. I remember Theo. Now, you have to go. Don't take anything, just go. And please take care of Alexander. I know you will, I always knew you would. You're the same person, you and him.

You'd die to protect the people you love, the both of you, that's why I sent him over to you. But don't get stupid with it. Just take care of him. And let him take care of you."

"Thank you," Miles breathed. "God, thank you."

"Go, Miles. The clock is ticking. I'll phone Jennifer to send a car to take you to the airport. I'm sorry you have to do this, but maybe – you haven't been happy in a long time. Maybe this won't be all terrible."

"Thank you, Jacob," Miles said, still in shock. "I'll call you when we're at yours."

"Delete Twitter and Instagram. Don't listen to your voicemail. Your phone is just a phone now, okay? It texts and it calls. That's it. Like the good old days," Jacob warned.

"Okay. Okay. I can do that. Fuck - okay. I'm going to – " Miles glanced at Alexander, at the way he'd gone pale and small. "I'm going to tell Alexander and then we're going to go. I guess. Thank you. God. I don't know – I don't know."

"They'll get her," Jacob promised. "In a way that counts. They'll get her. Don't think about it. Don't get in your head about it. Just go now. Miles, be safe. I care about you."

Jacob hung up the phone and Miles stared mutely at it.

"Samantha – " Alexander said, and Miles shook his head.

"Not in the way you're thinking, but something similar," Miles said. "We need to go. This apartment, it's not safe anymore. I'm sorry. I told you, I'm a spark. I burn things."

"Miles," Alexander said, closing his eyes for a few seconds like he was in pain. "You don't burn things. You're not burning me. This was always going to happen. Not to you, but to somebody. Even if I'd been celibate my entire life, even if I'd never looked at another person. It was an inevitability. It's all about power."

"Jacob says we run. To London. He has an apartment there. Would you do that with me? Could you do that with me? Because you don't have to. I know it's not ideal. It wouldn't be forever. It'd just be – a bolt hole," Miles said, and dipped his head forward, not wanting to meet Alexander's eyes.

Running away didn't feel like something to be proud of.

"Fuck, Miles. London sounds good, but are you sure? It sounds too easy. Fuck," Alexander said, and reached over and took Miles' hand gently. "I'm not blaming you for this. I don't even know if I'm blaming myself. It's her. She did this. I always knew she would and now she actually is, it's almost a relief."

"Because it's an ending," Miles said, remembering one of their conversations. "It means it ends."

"One way or another, it means it ends. We're not running, Miles. We're retreating. They're different things. I'll get my stuff. Give me ten minutes. I guess I was right about this place, huh?" Alexander sounded very far away, like he wasn't quite here. Miles looked at him.

"Are you with me, Alexander?"

Alexander stood, and nodded, leaning forward and pressing the smallest kiss to Miles' forehead. Miles' world tilted slightly and he leaned into it, gone before it was ever really there.

Miles let himself tip sideways on the floor as Alexander wandered around the apartment throwing stuff into a bag.

When the buzzer went to let them know the car was waiting for them, Alexander held out a hand to pull Miles up. They stood, looking at each other.

"I guess I'd go anywhere with you," Alexander said softly, seeming to take charge. Miles wondered how he could be so in control right now.

"That's lucky," Miles replied, just as soft. "Look, all of this, it's all for you, okay?"

The buzzer rang again.

"This isn't running away," Alexander reminded him.

"Okay," Miles said.

Alexander shouldered the bag, and reached out for Miles' hand with his other. Alexander didn't look back at the apartment as he pulled the door to. Miles did, and saw the leather jacket sitting there like an oil spill. How did that feel like half a lifetime ago?

*

The car ride to the airport felt like a liminal space, much like the one the night before, but the world had shifted and things weren't the

same anymore. They could never be the same.
And yet when Miles looked across at Alexander,
his heart still flipped in the exact same way.
More, perhaps. A steadier, more earthy kind of
feeling, something that was putting down roots.

God, he thought, *let this soil be rich.*

They hadn't spoken since leaving the apartment,
since leaving their lives behind. What could they
possibly say? The world was ending and they
were fleeing, not looking back at the explosion
of it.

Samantha - and it had to be her - because
nobody else could be so cruel, was trying to
destroy them, the fragile little thing that they'd
stumbled into. And Miles couldn't let her.

Miles, despite his upbringing, found it hard to
believe in justice these days. Being ripped to
shreds regularly for all the world to see had had
that effect on him. But he had to believe that this
was an ending. A full stop at the end of the
sentence. For Alexander's sake, it had to be.
He'd lived with it long enough.

Alexander was fiddling with the packet of pills,
and he hadn't taken any, Miles knew that. But he
kept running his fingers over the popped blisters
in a way that could only be interpreted as

wanting to. Miles wouldn't make that decision for him. That's not who Miles could, or should, be for him.

Before, before and before and before, Alexander had asked if there were two sides to this. There had always had to be, really. They were two people, after all. And as easy as it would be to fall into each other, Miles couldn't let that happen. It was self-destructive, it would be an act of sabotage. They could have something great, but it needed to be real.

This could be *something*, Miles knew that in his gut. But for the first time, he was willing to read the terms and conditions of it, the horrible small print that made things difficult. Miles wanted to love Alexander in a way that was informed and careful. He wanted to love him with his whole heart, but he didn't want to own him. He wanted to watch Alexander soar, he didn't want to cage him.

Alexander's eyes flicked over to his, and Alexander smiled, a little sad, a little tired.

"You still have your eyeliner on," Alexander said, and it was such an innocuous statement after so much brutality that Miles had to laugh. Alexander brightened with it, and shook his head. "This is ridiculous. This is all - it's ridiculous. I don't know how you do this."

"It's never been this bad before," Miles said, only that wasn't true. He'd just never let someone see it be this bad before.

"Yeah, it has," Alexander replied, seeming to read Miles' thoughts. "But it won't be, ever again. We don't let it. I can't watch you go through it now that I know you. You protected me. You're still protecting me. Let me protect you."

It could have felt like an empty gesture, because what could Alexander reasonably do? But Miles saw it for what it was: A promise. A future. The very deliberate use of *we*, that they *were* a they, an us. There was a path ahead, for them.

It could begin in London. Maybe they'd already begun walking it.

"This is messy," Miles said. "This is really messy."

"I shouldn't have said that," Alexander said, and sighed. "I knew I was hurting you when I said it. I know what people have called you, and I still said it. It was – the last chance I gave myself. To walk away. To see if you'd walk away. But we kept each other. So maybe I can handle messy, after all. Besides," Alexander paused, and held his hand out across the seats, palm up, bridging the gap between them once again and wiggling his fingers for Miles to take it. "If I have to do messy, I want to do it with you."

Miles took Alexander's hand, feeding off the warmth of it. It felt like the most real thing in the world.

"Aren't you scared?" Miles asked, feeling foolish, like a child.

"Yes," Alexander answered honestly. "I'm scared that I can't give you what you want. That I won't be enough. Like eventually the dam would burst. I'm scared that one day you'll touch me and my body will reject it. I'm scared of – everything, I think. But I've been scared for such a long time, Miles. I've spent seventeen years scared out of my mind. The guillotine has been swinging there, right above my neck, and I've been scared that it'll drop. Every fucking day. Scared to Google my name and scared not to. Scared isn't something novel to me. So yes, I'm scared, but don't think that makes you special. I get scared about going grocery shopping."

Miles didn't say anything. Couldn't say anything. He squeezed Alexander's hand and hoped that meant enough.

"I'm so glad I met you," Miles said, after several minutes of silence. "I don't know what to do with myself, sometimes. I look at you, god, I'm holding your hand. And I think to myself: after everything, what world thinks I deserve this? But it's you, isn't it? It's not the world who gets to decide. It's you. You think I deserve this. And I don't know what to do with that."

"You'll find the words," Alexander said. "You always have before. You will again."

"You want me to write songs about you?" Miles asked, surprised. He wouldn't have thought Alexander could ever want that, to be a doomed Miles Montgomery muse.

Alexander squeezed his hand this time.

"It's what you do, isn't it? And I don't say that to be flippant. It's who you are. It's in your blood, in your heartbeat. It goes to the foundations of you. I couldn't ask you not to. I wouldn't. And – I want to hear how you talk about us. The words you'll use. I want to listen to a song and know you cared enough to write it about me. It's vain, I know. But I think it's the best thing you could ever give me. The most honest thing. Your soul is in your music. So if you break a piece of it off for me, that – that's incredible. It means I've done something right."

"Nobody's ever said that about what I do before," Miles said.

"Nobody's ever listened properly before, then. I love Jacob, but he never listened. You don't hate the people you sing about, you love them. You immortalise them. You never tried to tear him down. You wrote about him because you loved him so much you couldn't not. That's who you are, Miles. You love things. So, so much."

Miles looked at their hands. Maybe, maybe he could let himself believe that.

*

Miles pulled his hoodie low over his forehead as he stepped out of the car at the airport, and Alexander bristled in much the same way that Miles felt. There was hopefully nobody to see them, they had driven pretty much straight in, but after everything, any eyes on them felt like too many.

They were guided to the plane and settled comfortably, and Miles was thankful for the first time in his life that he had access to a private plane. Alexander looked a little overwhelmed, and Miles didn't know what to say. He'd felt overwhelmed too, for the longest time. But at some point he'd stopped. How weird was that? He'd stopped being overwhelmed by the sheer amount of privilege he had. That the use of a private plane was not only normal, but expected.

Maybe he could start feeling a sense of awe about that again, but not today. Part of him, such a big part of him, would trade all of this in for something quieter, because it was exhausting. The wonder was gone. And that just felt sad.

How much had he lost without realising it? How much had been taken?

No, he couldn't let that happen anymore. Alexander sat awkwardly opposite him in the plush seat, and Miles nudged his knee under the table. The brief burst of contact grounded him, even as they readied themselves to take off.

"This is – a lot," Alexander said, voicing what Miles was thinking. "I knew, intellectually that you had a private plane, but actually being on one is – a lot."

"It's weird what you get used to," Miles said, looking around. He was drawn back to Alexander though, like a moth to the flame.

"This isn't what life is supposed to look like," Alexander said. "But you get that, right? This is isolation. Everything, it's all a trap to keep you separate. I can't imagine you living like this. Jacob should have – somebody should have done more. For you. Before it got to this. You must have been so lonely."

"It's just a plane," Miles said, though it wasn't. The engines started to rumble, and Alexander flinched.

"I hate this bit," he said, and Miles nudged his knee again.

"It'll be over in a minute," Miles said, looking out of the window. Soon, they'd be flying. Flying away. Somewhere new, somewhere old. A clash of past and present. He'd been happy in London with Jacob, before the world had turned on him. He could be happy with Alexander in a thousand different ways, and they were all waiting for him.

Alexander closed his eyes as the plane started to shake.

"Baby, I'm right here," Miles breathed, and Alexander's eyes opened, awed in a way Miles hadn't seen before, and Miles realised what he'd said. "I didn't mean to say that. I mean, I did, but not – not yet. It doesn't have to mean anything if you don't want it to," Miles apologised.

"Please mean it," Alexander said, and reached across the table to hold both of Miles' hands in his. The plane shuddered into the sky, and Alexander held on, and as Miles swallowed to try to stop his ears popping, he could hear his heart beating so damn fast, and yeah, he could mean it.

"Baby," he whispered again, and rubbed his thumb against the skin of Alexander's hand.

When Alexander smiled at him, it was open and wide, and as they climbed above the clouds, Miles believed in wonder again. Goddamn, he was going to live through this. He wanted to make Alexander smile like that every day.

That felt like a gift.

It had never been about who they'd moulded him into. It had been about waiting. And he'd waited. And now, Alexander was here.

The rest was details. A tangled ball of string they could spend the rest of their lives unravelling.

"You're thinking really hard," Alexander said, a little concerned.

"Only good things," Miles promised.

It was so blue outside, and Miles had never looked properly before. The kind of blue that didn't seem real. The whole world was beneath them, and they were suspended, above it all, and that should have been terrifying, but for the first time in a long time, Miles was just excited.

*

Somehow, they managed to sleep in shifts throughout the eight hour flight, checking in with each other as they inched closer to their destination, checking the flight tracker and counting down the miles. Miles felt an anticipation he hadn't felt for a long time, and Alexander just looked more alive than Miles had ever seen him.

"You keep looking at me," Alexander said, observing.

"I think I'm waiting to wake up," Miles admitted. "This all feels too surreal. The video shoot, everything, it all feels like something I could have dreamt up. It doesn't feel like a real thing that happened."

"I know how that feels," Alexander said, and rubbed his thumb across Miles' knuckles. "Like everything is slightly left of where it should be. And you keep hoping it'll shift back and it never does. So you learn to live with the world being slightly wrong, until you barely notice it at all, until you wake up one day and it's gone back to normal. And then normal seems all wrong."

"You've really lived it, haven't you? Every inch of it. I can look at you and almost forget. And I know I need to, because I can't swaddle you in bubble wrap and treat you like you're something breakable. I know you're the same asshole you've always been. I know that. But you've fought your war, too, haven't you? You've really been there," Miles said, and shook his head.

"Don't treat me like I'm fragile. Even when I am. I can't cope with that. I need you to treat me like you always have. I can't have you look at me like I'm about to break. Not when we're this close to making it out alive. To use your analogy, yeah, I fought, for a long time. I'm still fighting. Shellshock, you know?" Alexander sighed heavily.

"That's what they called it before they called it PTSD. I know I have that. But that's not all that I am, nor is it all that I want to be. I told you everything because I trusted you to see past that. I know you do. I know this is a lot to navigate. We're both going to make mistakes. You've fought your battles too, far more publicly than me. It's not a competition. We're wounded, both of us. But we can heal. London, Miles, we're going to London. I've never been. I've been so many places, but never London. This is new. Untainted. I want it to be something good. I want to let it be something good. Yeah?" Alexander looked at Miles, his eyes reflecting the skies outside, turning them a different shade of green that Miles couldn't put a name to.

"You talk more now," Miles said. "When we met, I thought you were sort of – solemn. Quiet. But that's not it at all, is it? You're an open book, you always have been. People just don't know how to read you. They've looked at you, but never really seen you."

"You see me. You read me. You're a wordsmith. It's what you're best at," Alexander said.

"You're a language I didn't know I could speak," Miles admitted.

"You should write that down, that's good. I like that," Alexander said.

"You're going to be a terrible enabler, aren't you? You're using me for my songs. I knew it. You're only dating me for the clout," Miles teased.

"Am I dating you?" Alexander asked, smirk on his face, and Miles considered for a moment.

"Since the first second, baby. You and me, no matter what we said to each other. The lies we told to try to escape it, we could never have been anything else."

"I still don't know how to do this," Alexander said, and Miles shrugged, looking at the city coming into view beneath them.

"Haven't you heard? I'm an expert at this. I know all the tricks."

"I don't need tricks," Alexander said, and followed Miles' gaze out of the window. "I only need you. Nothing more fancy than that. I need to be able to keep up, after all."

"You're doing just fine," Miles said. "Definitely top five."

"You're the worst," Alexander said, grinning, still holding Miles' hands in his.

"But you're dating me, so. Jacob was right, you do have appalling taste."

"Me and him have that in common then," Alexander said and shrugged lopsided, like he really didn't care.

"It's not weird for you, me and him?" Miles asked.

"He's not the one sitting here with you now, is he?" Alexander asked, and squeezed Miles' hands.

"Very manly, I like it," Miles replied, and grinned a little wider.

"Fuck off," Alexander muttered, but he was still smiling.

"I think you're stuck with me. Talk about a poor life choice," Miles pointed out.

"I regret everything," Alexander deadpanned, trying for bland, but he couldn't keep the genuine happiness out of his voice. Miles could hear the way it shone.

*

PART II

Chapter Eight

@BUZZFEED: WHERE DID THEY GO? RADIO SILENCE FROM MALEX! TWEET YOUR TOP CONSPIRACY THEORIES!

I didn't know I could speak you

Until I wrapped you around my tongue

Didn't know how to see you

Until I looked into your eyes

You're the sunset in purples

And baby, you're sunrise

You're yesterday, today

And goddamn, you're my tomorrow too

I want to be messy with you.

- *Messy, Miles Montgomery*

*

They arrived at the apartment and it was somehow still afternoon, like time has stopped and given them a grace period before deciding to start up again.

Miles keyed in the gate code and pushed the heavy iron gate open, before wandering down the concrete slope to where the apartment was. It was completely unassuming, it didn't look like a famous person's apartment block, it was just – normal.

Miles once again resisted the urge to kick the ugly gnome, though he could see even Alexander giving it the side-eye as he lifted it. It was weirdly light, like Miles had suspected, as he grabbed the keys from beneath it.

"Silver key downstairs, gold key upstairs, Miles repeated to himself, and tried the lock. "Okay, no, gold key downstairs, silver key upstairs." The door finally clicked open, and they looked at the endless amount of stairs in front of them.

"Jacob doesn't believe in elevators, huh?" Alexander commented.

Miles huffed, remembering that argument.

"He does not," he said.

Somehow climbing the surprisingly steep stairs to the second storey was the breaking point for Miles' exhaustion, and by the time he was outside of Jacob's front door, all he wanted to do was sleep for a week. The blue sky outside the window mocked him.

"I'm suddenly so tired," Alexander said, echoing his thoughts.

"Evil stairs," Miles said. "Like, we should get a young priest and an old priest kinda evil."

"Maybe tomorrow?" Alexander all but whined. "I need to sleep." He leant his body heavily against Miles' back as Miles tried to remember which key he was supposed to be using. Alexander seemed calmer about instigating touch, and he didn't particularly seem to mind the subtle touches Miles had offered either. Miles couldn't allow himself to be too hopeful, they were both giddy and exhausted after everything that had happened, neither of them thinking too clearly.

But Miles allowed himself to be a little hopeful, nonetheless.

Jacob's flat was as Miles remembered it, though with a different couch and a larger television. Someone obviously came in every so often to dust, though the collection of plants Jacob had once cultivated had all been removed at some point. There sat instead one lonely cactus that seemed to be tenaciously holding onto life.

"Oh, lonely cactus," Miles sang, and poked at it. "Oww."

He sucked his finger into his mouth, and looked around at Alexander, who was laughing at him gently.

"I'm really tired, okay," he said around it, and Alexander only laughed harder. It was a brilliant sound, and Miles would poke all the cacti in the world to get that sound out of Alexander again.

"Is this yours?" Alexander asked, and pointed to something that was so familiar to Miles that he hadn't acknowledged it as notable. It was his old guitar, one of his first guitars, a nothing-special electro-acoustic purple baby covered in stickers, that had probably cost a fraction of the guitars he owned now. It was perched in its stand, and aside from a small layer of dust, was exactly how Miles remembered it.

"Holy shit," Miles breathed. "I assumed he like, bulldozed it or something. I don't know, swift violent death. I was not kind to him with that guitar, not towards the end. I – wow. Okay, memories."

Miles stepped forward and stroked the strings, and they let out an awful discordant sound.

"Okay, it is very out of tune, but I swear, I loved this guitar."

"You'll have to play something for me," Alexander said, standing close to Miles again, gravitating into his orbit.

Miles yawned. "Can I slip into a coma first? Just like, a small one. Six to eight months, nothing major."

"We should probably eat," Alexander suggested. He was right. They'd eaten on the plane, but even private planes didn't have *nice* food. Miles whined, even as Alexander moved away to check the takeaway menus on the fridge. "Chinese?"

"I literally do not care. I am so beyond caring. Just put something in my stomach that's vaguely edible," Miles said, not really caring that he sounded whiny.

"Poor baby," Alexander said, and turned on his phone, swiping away the notifications, and making the call.

"How come when I say it you light up, but when you say it I feel faintly patronised?" Miles said, and Alexander held a finger to his lips, before placing the order. Miles' mouth watered as Alexander reeled off a long list of food items.

Alexander ended the call and looked at Miles, crowding in close, pressing a kiss to the small raven's peak of Miles' hairline.

"Baby," he said, and Miles shivered.

"Okay, maybe it still works when you say it," Miles admitted.

"I thought it might," Alexander said, then looked surprised at himself. "God, it's – it's not even a comfort zone thing, it's just weird that I get to call somebody that. That I get to call *you* that."

"We need to make a list. Of things that are okay and not okay. That should be – " Miles muffled a yawn unsuccessfully, "that should be a priority. Because we're grownups and if this is going to be a thing, we need," he waved his arm, trying to think of the word with his foggy brain, "boundaries."

"I agree," Alexander said. "But can we not do it in front of the Chinese? I just want to eat and sleep and maybe at some stage figure out what the fuck is happening with my life. Then we can figure out – logistics."

"You chose the least sexy term on purpose," Miles said, and Alexander hummed in the back of his throat.

"Don't want to get your hopes up," Alexander said softly, bringing the mood back down to earth. Because, yeah, that was fair.

"You're not," Miles said. "If this is all we get, I'm happy with that. I don't want to ever do anything you're not comfortable with."

*

"I'm really uncomfortable with the way you're using those chopsticks," Alexander remarked. "I'm pretty sure they're not for stabbing."

Miles waved a chopstick at Alexander threateningly, still chewing his noodles.

"They can be for stabbing, Alexander Raine. Nobody knows where you are, don't tempt me."

"Getting murdered by Miles Montgomery would make me famous forever, I think," Alexander said. "That'd kind of suck. Don't do that."

"Baby, I could never murder you," Miles promised.

"And they say romance is dead."

Miles picked up a noodle and threw it at him, revelling in the very unmanly squeak Alexander produced as it slid down his cheek.

*

"So Jacob only has one bedroom," Miles said, tossing the waste from the Chinese into the bin. "But I figured I could sleep on the couch. I mean, last time I was here it was a foldout one, but, eh. This one looks comfortable enough. He has spare blankets, it'll be fine."

"You can't sleep on the couch," Alexander argued.

"Well I don't really see any other options, realistically. I'm not going to force myself into bed with you. That's not fair. Not after everything," Miles argued back.

"Let me take the couch then," Alexander said, tiredness making him grouchy, arms crossed across his chest, voice gravelly.

"No. I'm not going to do that."

"Then share the bed with me. Miles, I can handle sharing a bed for fuck's sake," Alexander growled, more at himself than at Miles. Miles put his hands up to placate him.

"I know you can baby, but have you ever? What if it's not something you can – cope with? I don't want to push this but last night, the night before? I don't know, time zones, but you know. You told me the worst stuff I'd ever heard and I don't want to – amplify that."

"You're amplifying it right now, by not just acting like a normal human being around me," Alexander huffed, and turned away, slouching over to the couch. He laid down on it like he meant to stay the night, crossing his arms over his chest.

Miles moved over to kneel beside Alexander's head, and laced his fingers between Alexander's. God, he'd put him through so much in such a short space of time.

"I'm sorry. It's been – it's *been*, you know. I'm not always going to know the right thing to say."

Alexander looked at him, before pulling Miles' hand close enough that he could kiss the knuckles, a butterfly kiss to each one.

"Can we just try it? Please. If I don't like it, I'll tell you," Alexander promised.

"I'm keeping my clothes on," Miles said. Alexander grinned, and rolled his eyes.

"So sexy right now," he joked, and Miles nudged his chest with the hand Alexander was still holding.

"He makes jokes," Miles said.

"He does," Alexander replied.

"Bed, then?" Miles asked, and Alexander squeezed his hand a little tighter than normal. Like he was nervous. He probably was, Miles realised. And rightly so. Miles could sleep pretty much anywhere, with anybody, but Alexander had never had the opportunity to get used to that. It was going to be a learning curve. "I don't snore. I have it on good authority. There have been many things I've done in bed, but I've never snored. Really good, like, septum, you know. For singing. Good airways. So no snoring."

"I don't know if I snore," Alexander said, looking puzzled, and that made sense, if he'd never shared a bed, he couldn't know if he snored or not. He'd never had anyone to tell him either way.

"Then I get to learn something brand new about you that even you don't know," Miles said, and copied Alexander's earlier movement, pulling Alexander's knuckles to his lips and kissing them gently. "I think you're still trying to scare me away. It's not working."

Miles pulled at Alexander's hand, and groaning, Alexander got up off the couch.

"Do you want the bathroom first, or?" Miles asked. "Jacob was always pretty good about the spare toothbrushes thing, I'm assuming that hasn't changed."

"Yeah, I'll – I'll go first. Another new thing for me," Alexander said.

"Really just knocking them out of the park today, and it's not even evening yet," Miles remarked.

Alexander squeezed Miles' hand again before dropping it.

"You're something else, Miles," he said, and headed off to the bathroom.

Miles took the opportunity to survey the bedroom, to pull the blinds, and shake out the blankets, coughing a little as a fine layer of dust floated into the air. It'd have to do for tonight, they could worry about laundry tomorrow.

Alexander emerged, and he'd taken off his t-shirt, just in a black tank top and his jeans.

"Are you going to be able to sleep in those?" Miles asked. Alexander looked down.

"I didn't bring anything else with me. I didn't really – I wasn't really thinking. I did not pack well." He chewed his lip nervously.

"The couch is still an option, for me, I mean," Miles said, giving Alexander an out.

"No, it's okay, just, can you be in the bathroom whilst I get changed?" Alexander asked, and it was such an easy thing for Miles to agree to that his heart nearly broke as he nodded and Alexander looked relieved.

Miles busied himself in the bathroom, thankful he'd worn sweatpants. He kept his t-shirt on too, thankful it wasn't too warm. He was right about Jacob's supply of toothbrushes, and stole some of his toothpaste to brush his teeth. There were still remnants of eyeliner circling his eyes, and he rubbed at it, but it seemed pretty stuck there. A problem for the morning. Jacob would definitely have makeup remover somewhere. Miles looked forward to rifling through his stuff to find it.

Miles stood in the bathroom for longer than he needed to, trying to listen to hear if Alexander had gotten into the bed. He hoped Alexander wasn't putting on a brave face. But he had to trust him. He had to let Alexander make his own choices.

Finally, he left the bathroom and walked into the bedroom, where Alexander was indeed propped up against the headboard, the lamp on beside him, reading the back of a book, wearing thick framed glasses.

"Oh, I forgot about Jacob's weird bedside library," Miles mused. "And can I just take a moment to say that you look ridiculously good in glasses? I have been trying so hard not to objectify you, but you're making it really, really difficult right now."

Alexander grinned, and pushed the glasses up his nose a little.

"You're allowed to look, Miles. I work hard for this body. I'm not going to tell you that you can't look. I trust you. You've been the perfect gentleman."

"I didn't say anything about your body," Miles pointed out. "I was only talking about your glasses. But if I'm allowed to mention your body, then – "

"Miles, get in the bed," Alexander interrupted. "You can objectify me tomorrow."

"Ooh, promises, promises," Miles said, but pushed back the blankets to slide in. It was a big bed, so they weren't even close to touching. There was a veritable canyon of distance between them.

"I'm going to read for a bit, are you okay with the lamp?" Alexander asked, and Miles nodded, pulling the pillow down to beat it into comfortable submission. He thought back to his pillow at home, and missed it. Alexander wouldn't have mocked it. Probably. Maybe a little. But he'd have understood.

Miles didn't think he'd be able to sleep, but somewhere between the slow slide of Alexander turning the pages, and the steady in and out of Alexander's breathing, Miles couldn't keep his eyes open any longer. The lamp was still on, casting shadows against the wall, as he drifted into unconsciousness.

Chapter Nine

Miles woke in the darkness to someone shaking him. It took him a few seconds to orientate himself and remember where he was. It was Alexander shaking him. He was in Jacob's apartment, in London. They were safe.

"Miles," Alexander said, hushed. "Miles, come look."

A shriek pierced the night air, and Miles remembered that noise. Foxes.

"I've seen them, wake me up when it's wolves," he mumbled, and tried to bury his face back in the pillow, which he noticed belatedly, was Alexander's. At some point, he'd made his way across the bed, and was now very much on Alexander's side. If Alexander minded, he wasn't saying anything.

"Miles, there're babies," Alexander said, and prodded Miles' shoulder, and Miles groaned.

"You could have led with that," he said, and rubbed the sleep from his eyes, getting up gently, as though he could scare the fox cubs away with his footsteps alone. Alexander made his way back to where he'd opened the blinds a little, and Miles joined him, and from the light of a streetlamp, they could make out three fox cubs and one proud parent, gambolling around on the flat roof opposite Jacob's window.

"They're playing," Alexander said, not taking his eyes off them. As Miles watched, one of the cubs nipped at another's tail, then ran away as it turned, so its sibling got the furry blame instead.

"It played a trick!" Miles exclaimed, delightedly. "Did you see that?"

"I saw," Alexander said, fondly.

"Thank you for waking me," Miles said. "Sorry I was grumpy."

"It's okay," Alexander said, not watching the foxes now, but looking at Miles. Miles looked back at him, at the shadows of his face, the way the light outside cast him in orange and black.

Alexander's eyes flicked to Miles' lips then back up to his eyes. Miles licked his lips subconsciously. He watched Alexander's eyes follow the movement.

"I don't know – " Alexander said, and made a small noise in the back of his throat, before stepping closer to Miles, impossibly close, so Miles could feel the heat radiating off him, less than an inch separating them. "I don't know if I'm doing the right thing or not. I don't know how to make these choices. But I really, really want to kiss you right now."

"For what it's worth," Miles said, and found he was whispering, "I really, really want you to."

"I might not be good at it," Alexander warned, ghosting ever closer, his breathing little puffs against Miles' mouth.

"Everyone's good at kissing," Miles said, low and breakable, hushed by the darkness.

Alexander closed the gap between them, impossibly slow, and placed the smallest kiss on Miles' lips before pulling away. They stared at each other for a long moment, before Alexander closed the gap again, and this time there was nothing soft about it. His lips moved against Miles' in a way that was unpractised, but deliberate. Miles couldn't help but shudder with it. This was more intimate than anything he could have imagined doing with Alexander, and as Alexander's hands found his hips and pulled him closer still. He whimpered against Alexander's mouth, and Alexander took it as an opportunity to slide his tongue into Miles' mouth, and it was like Alexander was learning him, through every noise Miles made, by the way his body was reacting, by the way Miles' hands snaked up Alexander's back and held him close.

Alexander pulled back, and years could have gone past, all in the blink of an eye. Miles felt claimed, felt protected, felt *loved*.

"I have to stop," Alexander breathed out, and he didn't sound upset, more flustered. "I have to stop or we're going to end up doing something we're not ready for."

"That's – wow. Okay," Miles said, and nodded. Alexander pressed one last kiss to the corner of Miles' mouth, before pushing him back against the bed, hands still on Miles' hips.

"I don't know what to do with you," Alexander said, and shook his head. His eyes were so dark, blown wide. "I didn't think I could want this."

"You can do anything," Miles breathed. "Anything, I swear."

Another shriek, outside, the cubs still playing.

"They're supposed to be trickster spirits, you know," Alexander said, voice still quiet, still speaking his words onto Miles' skin. "I don't know how I know that, but I read it somewhere."

"They're noisy," Miles said.

"God, Miles, so are you," Alexander said, and Miles felt himself flush. "I didn't know I could make someone do that."

"You're going to have to stop talking, or I'm going to have to excuse myself, and it won't be dignified," Miles admitted.

Alexander's hands dropped reluctantly from Miles' hips, and Miles slid his hands down Alexander's back before dropping them to his sides.

"You're shaking," Alexander said, and Miles hadn't realised he was.

"Adrenaline," Miles said. "Happens sometimes. Not for a long time. I don't know if it's part of the ADHD or if it's just a me thing. Normally means something really good is happening to me."

Alexander stepped back, and it looked like it took all of his willpower.

"You have no idea what you do to me," Alexander said. "What you make me want to do."

"You can. You only need to ask," Miles said. "Whatever you want."

"Get back into bed, Miles," Alexander said softly. "Or I'm going to have to excuse myself."

Miles tingled all over, but he did as Alexander said, pulling the blankets over him. Alexander looked back out the window one last time before pulling the blankets back and getting into the bed.

"We were pretty close when I woke up," Miles said. "I didn't – I'm a bit of an octopus, I should have warned you. I didn't think."

"You kick, too," Alexander said, and Miles could hear the smile in his voice. "Now come here."

Alexander reached out his arm and used it to pull Miles close to him. Miles ended up with his head cushioned on Alexander's chest, ear just over his heart.

"Your heart's beating so fast," Miles murmured.

Alexander ran his fingers through Miles' hair, and Miles about melted.

"Must mean something good's happening," Alexander said, and Miles started to fall asleep again, to that slightly too fast beat.

Something good *was* happening. Miles breathed in the smell of Alexander, cologne and musk and the hint of sweat and stale air from the plane.

"You kissed me," Miles said, muffled, barely there.

"Yeah," Alexander said. "I did."

"We should do that again. For science."

"Go to sleep, Miles," Alexander said, running his finger down to Miles' earlobe then along the tufts of his hairline. Miles sighed sleepily, a long exhale that felt like it'd been a long time coming, and let himself enjoy the sensation. He could sleep, for a little while.

Alexander would be there when he woke up.

*

Miles woke up before Alexander, legs tangled together, and with one arm thrown over Alexander's stomach, and as much as he didn't want to move, after a couple of minutes of staring at Alexander sleeping, he shook himself, telling himself not to invade on this, and, as quietly as he could, rolled out of the bed and slouched off to look for coffee.

When he reached the strange little open plan kitchen, living room, he couldn't help but get drawn back to that purple guitar; just sitting there, untuned but still bearing all the sticker scars of twenty two year old Miles Montgomery. Gently, he lifted it from its stand, and strummed the strings again, wincing, before beginning to tune it, one string at a time, bringing it back home to him.

The guitar felt good in his hands, something solid and real and like belonging. His fingers played through a few chords, idly, without thinking about it, and he thought about Alexander, who was sleeping in the bedroom a few feet away, and he could only imagine the songs he could write if he gave himself permission.

Alexander had given him permission though, hadn't he? Couldn't that be enough, for now?

Miles reached for where he'd left his phone on the arm of the couch, and turned it on, swiping away the notifications without even looking.

He'd remembered to text Jacob the day before, to let him know they'd arrived safely, but he didn't need to see Jacob's reply, not yet. He felt like they were in a bubble, him and Alexander, and the rest of the world could wait its turn.

Miles thought back to bathtubs and pill packets and then shook his head. That could all wait. He wanted to write about the good before the bad, he wanted to write about fox cubs and first kisses and the temptation to do so much more. He wanted to write about coming home after being away for such a long time, and not realising home wasn't where he'd thought it could be.

He pressed the record button on his phone, and started to strum the guitar, humming to himself, small snatches of lyrics sneaking in as he ran his left hand up and down the fret board, fingertips beginning to ache in that way that was so satisfying.

It was mostly nonsense, it was stream of consciousness and it was scratchings on a chalkboard, but it wasn't nothing. It was more than he'd wanted to write for a long time. He lost himself in it, the guitar something akin to a weapon, except, no it wasn't that at all. When could a gun not be a gun? Alexander had said he wrote everything with love, and Miles had never considered that before. Maybe he wasn't leaving bullet holes in his wake, but tiny love letters.

He played until he had most of a chorus and two verses, nothing as ordered as he'd like, but still *something*. And then he tapped the button to stop recording, set the guitar down, stretched, and looked up.

Alexander stood in the doorway, sleep mussed and somehow more perfect than he'd ever looked, his stubble longer now and somehow softer for it, his face open from just waking up, his eyes bright even though Miles could see the sleep still nestled in the corners of them.

"How long have you been standing there?" Miles asked, and Alexander just smiled.

"Long enough," he said. "I wasn't wrong, was I?"

"About what?" Miles asked.

"About you. About the fact that you love what you write about. God, Miles, watching you – your craft, watching you find the words and put them together. It felt holy."

Miles blushed, and looked down at his phone, picking it up, then putting it down again.

"I think that's blasphemy," he said.

"I don't think I care," Alexander replied, and then yawned, the yawn resonating through the entirety of him. "Tell me there's coffee."

"I think there is, I hope so," Miles said, and stood, and made to walk past Alexander to the kitchen, but Alexander snagged his waist on the way past.

"Kiss?" Alexander asked, and Miles felt warm inside, like a furnace had been lit in his belly. He nodded, and Alexander leaned in, and Miles didn't care about morning breath or anything, because Alexander was kissing him, soft, gentle kisses that began on his lips, but moved slowly across his cheek, and then followed the line of his jawbone down, inching onto the soft skin below his chin, then onto his neck.

"Hey," Miles greeted him, when Alexander pulled back, and pressed a kiss to the end of Alexander's nose.

"Hey, yourself," Alexander replied.

"I could get used to this," Miles said, and couldn't help but reach out to touch Alexander's cheek, to rub at the grown out stubble there.

"Get used to it," Alexander said, and leant into Miles' touch like a cat. "I want to figure you out. Every inch of you. Get you to make those noises again."

"Could take a long time," Miles said, suddenly breathless.

"I'm counting on it," Alexander said, and let him go, headed for the kitchen, stretching to check the cupboards for an errant bag of coffee. Miles just watched him, head spinning slightly, feeling both unmoored and so desperately held close.

Alexander looked over his shoulder at him, and raised an eyebrow. Miles raised one back. Alexander smiled a little wider, and went back to searching for coffee. Miles let himself soak it all in, the impossible reality of it all. He watched the way Alexander's shoulder muscles moved and pulled as he pushed things aside and reached for the higher cupboards, and he *wanted*.

"I know you're staring," Alexander said without turning around, jolting Miles out of his reverie. "Which is very flattering, but a little help would also be appreciated. Plus, you're far too far away."

Miles stepped closer, and nudged Alexander's shoulder with his own before opening the next cupboard along.

"I'm right here," Miles said, and then made a sound of delight as he found the coffee bag sitting there. "Alexander?" He asked.

"Hmm?"

"How out of date is too out of date, do you think? Like, is two years bad?"

Alexander closed his own cupboard, and turned to rest his head on Miles' shoulder, moaning a little sadly.

"Don't make me go grocery shopping before I've had coffee, baby," he said.

"The world is crueller than we know," Miles agreed.

Alexander made a muffled noise of complaint and turned his face into Miles' throat, burying it there.

Miles thought back to his apartment in New York, at how he could phone someone and get whatever he wanted delivered to him at any hour of the day. But Alexander was nipping tiny kisses onto his throat now, and Miles stretched his neck to allow him access. Maybe it wasn't all bad, maybe un-caffeinated grocery runs could be – nice. He bit back a moan as Alexander scraped his teeth across his jaw.

He could definitely get used to this.

*

Alexander slid his reading glasses onto Miles' face, and stood back, grinning.

"There you go, Superman," he said, and Miles scrunched up his face.

"You are blind as fuck, what the hell," Miles said and peered blearily at Alexander, blinking quickly.

"I'm going to take that as a compliment," Alexander said, and smoothed a hand through his hair, looking in the hallway mirror.

"Don't," Miles replied. "Do you even have eyes?"

"You're terrible and I don't know why I put up with you," Alexander said, and nudged the back of Miles' head with his forehead. "And I know you like my eyes. Enough to sing about them, at least. Now please, can we get some coffee or we will have bigger problems than my poor eyesight."

Miles pulled his hood up, and suddenly he looked like someone else, especially with the subtle five o'clock shadow reluctantly growing in.

"What if they recognise us?" He asked, and Alexander pressed a kiss to his nape, wrapping his arms around to link in front of Miles' navel.

"They won't. I'm not actually a big deal, and you don't even look like you. Plus, from what I've learnt from Jacob, British people are astonishingly good at not giving a fuck."

Miles turned in Alexander's embrace, and kissed Alexander once, twice, three times for luck.

"This is shockingly domestic," he said, and then wriggled free, Alexander pretending like he wouldn't let him go. "Going grocery shopping together."

"Be romantic after coffee, baby," Alexander said, and put a hand on Miles' shoulder to steer him towards the door.

"I can be romantic at all phases of coffee-having," Miles grumbled. "You're just emotionally dead inside."

"Oh, so you've talked to my therapist," Alexander joked, and Miles grinned.

"You think you're funny, and it's going to break my heart to tell you you're not. You'll be a husk of a man, stripped of his one personality trait. This is your villain origin story."

"You're going to be my villain origin story if I don't get caffeine soon," Alexander growled, and Miles grabbed the keys.

"We're going, we're going," Miles muttered, and slipped his hand into Alexander's.

They left the apartment, a vague idea of where they were going, and with the hope the British public would leave them alone.

*

The British public not only left them alone, but seemed to actively shun them.

"God, I'd forgotten what Londoners were like," Miles said, dodging between the crowds of people, both hands weighed down with grocery bags. "They literally don't care if you live or die."

"I'm really worried that Jacob is the nicest of them, and he's awful," Alexander replied.

"We've mellowed him. We're good people. If he didn't know us, he'd probably be even worse," Miles said, and took a passing briefcase to the knee. "Fuck."

"Maybe we can get home deliveries from now on," Alexander said, though he looked brighter now he'd ducked into a Starbucks and had a coffee cup in his hand, balancing a grocery bag on his arm so he could sip from it.

"That sounds like a plan. God, we are good at this. We should do this professionally," Miles said.

"We're hiding from the international news media, in a foreign country, because somebody from my past has a vendetta against us and won't stop until we're destroyed," Alexander pointed out. "We're not great at this."

"But we bought two different types of bread. Without even crying. I've never managed that before," Miles pouted. "Food just kind of –

appears for me. I don't think I've been to a grocery store since I was seventeen."

"I'm very proud of you, really, baby, but I did have to drag you away from the chocolate aisle. That kind of undermines your point a little."

"I need to prove to you that Jacob is wrong and that British chocolate is superior," Miles said.

Alexander looked at him, and grinned, that soft little grin Miles couldn't quite categorise.

"You remember that?" Alexander asked.

The thing is, Miles did. He remembered pretty much everything they'd ever said to each other, like he'd pressed record on an old cassette player somewhere and now he had it all stored, forever.

"Yeah, I remember," he said softly.

And that meant Alexander remembered, too.

Miles' heart fluttered in his chest, and it felt like butterflies, baby birds, maybe those terrifying extinct insects that were six feet across that had thankfully died out with the dinosaurs. There was a lot going on.

They reached the apartment door.

Miles fumbled for the keys.

"Okay, it's definitely silver key downstairs, gold key upstairs," he mumbled, mostly to himself. He tried it. "Oh, what the fuck, how can I be wrong every time, that's just against the rules of averages!"

Alexander poked Miles' cheek with his finger. "You're lucky you're pretty," he said.

"I'm Miles fucking Montgomery, you're lucky to have me," Miles said tartly, but with a smile plastered across his face.

"I do have you, don't I?" Alexander asked, and there was that small smile again, dancing in his eyes.

"Yeah, you do," Miles said, and finally got the door unlocked, shouldering it open. "Now do you think there are some local exorcists who can help with this stairs situation?"

"I think at some point you got really confused between architects and exorcists, but we can check," Alexander said.

"You really aren't as funny as you think you are," Miles lied.

"And yet somehow I think I'll survive," Alexander shrugged, and started climbing the stairs two at a time, like a total overachiever.

"Urghhhhhh," Miles groaned, and followed him, not actually minding the view he got of Alexander's ass in quite tight jeans.

"I'm objectifying you!" Miles called, as Alexander turned the first landing corner.

He heard Alexander bark a laugh in response, and smiled to himself.

This was good.

Chapter Ten

@MilesMontgomery: My boyfriend prefers Lindt to Cadburys therefore I'm considering a divorce.

@jacobcamden: @MilesMontgomery I'm stealing him.

*

And life continued to be good, settling into a kind of easy pattern, demanding little of them, Miles would write music, Alexander would crowd into him to kiss him, they'd watch the fox cubs play when they couldn't sleep, and the outside world left them alone. Miles began to realise he was writing an album. Something coherent, not just snippets of ideas anymore.

"I need to call Theo," he told Alexander, lazing in his arms on the couch, Netflix asking them if they were still there. "He's the best producer I know. I want to make this a thing. I know we're – hiding. But I want to make music. I feel like I'm going to explode with it. Like I need to do this. All these songs, they need to exist in the world. I need to make them exist. I don't know – god, I need to call Jennifer. Get a record label on board, I need to – I don't even know. But I want to tell the world about us. But that's really scary. Because we're really good, aren't we?"

Miles scanned Alexander's face, checking for a reaction. Alexander bit his lip, obviously thinking hard, brow furrowed. Miles found he couldn't stop talking.

"We're really, really good. We're happy. And I don't want to invite everyone to speculate on that. But I don't know how else to make things."

"Calm down," Alexander said softly, and pressed a kiss to Miles' temple. "I knew what I was signing up for. Or I know now, at least. I told you, it's okay. You won't ruin this. I promise. Your songs are incredible, baby, they deserve to be heard. Just – I don't know, don't give them everything. I know you want to – it's what you do, it's what you're born to do. Just, run stuff by me, maybe?"

"You know what Jacob went through," Miles said. "It took him years to shake me."

"And he's letting you stay in his apartment indefinitely," Alexander pointed out. "I think he's okay with you."

"I don't want you to have to forgive me," Miles said.

"Then ask for permission first. Like you always, always do. Ask me if I want to share this with you," Alexander said, like it was simple.

"Can I do this? Can I write an album about you?" Miles asked, and Alexander looked at him for a long time, like he was trying to figure him out.

"Isn't that what you've been doing since we got here? Since that very first morning? I told you, it's okay. You have my permission. My consent. Just – no break up songs, okay?"

"No break up songs," Miles agreed, and snuggled closer to Alexander. "You're stuck with me."

*

The next morning, Miles texted both Theo and Jennifer, entirely forgetting the five hour time difference. Theo was quicker to forgive than Jennifer, but he managed to talk them both round.

By the end of the week, Jennifer had talked to Universal, and it looked like they were on board. Theo was going to fly out with his wife Eiko to help Miles put an album together.

And Alexander?

Alexander seemed enthralled by the entire process, watching Miles work, taking videos on his phone of Miles playing around on his guitar. Jokingly, Miles had pulled Alexander over to that battered purple guitar and arranged his fingers on the frets, strumming out his first few chords. It hadn't come naturally to Alexander the way it did to Miles, but it felt like something, something they could share.

Once a week, Miles would find him glued to the television with a laptop set up on a Zoom call with Jacob, watching University Challenge and calling out the answers, getting a surprising number of them right. Miles would tease him about how smart he was, until it felt less like teasing and more like a fact they should do something with.

It felt like they were moving forward in a way Miles could have never imagined. Like a wall was crumbling that they'd refused to acknowledge. When they kissed, always with Alexander's gentle instigation, hands had started to wander a little more, and there was no more discreet excusing from situations when things got too heated, just harsh breaths and foreheads pressed together, eyes meeting, acknowledging, *soon*.

Soon.

*

Miles woke up hard, pressed against Alexander, the morning light filtering through the blinds.

Normally, he'd roll out of bed and take care of it in the shower, or just wait for it to go away, but Alexander reached behind him and grabbed his wrist as he made to move away.

"Stay," Alexander said, his voice sleep rough. "I want to watch you."

Miles eyesight sharpened immediately, his brain taking in Alexander's words and forcing him into full consciousness, and what had been something he could have ignored turned throbbing and desperate. Alexander rolled over, and looked at him, intense, searing, and Miles swallowed hard, his throat bobbing.

"Yeah?" Miles asked, looking for any sign of worry, or hesitation, or anxiety in Alexander's face. There was none. Alexander looked – he looked the way he did every time things got heated lately: like he wanted to push a little more, determined to cross the line but not sure how to. Miles had waited, patient, not wanting to demand too much.

Alexander nodded, and Miles pushed the blankets down, revealing his tented boxers.

"How?" He asked, and Alexander's eyes snapped from his groin to his face then back again.

"Christ," Alexander said, and shook his head, before pushing down the blankets himself, revealing himself to be equally hard. "I don't care, I just need to see you."

"You want this?" Miles said, having to check, even as all his blood seemed to be draining away from his brain and the heat pooled in his stomach.

Alexander sat up, and in one fluid motion, swung a leg over Miles', so that he was straddling just above his knees, resting his weight on Miles' thighs. It was an incredible sight to behold, and Alexander had long since foregone wearing a tank top to bed, so Miles could take him in, reaching out a hand to trail down those abs, softer than they had been, weeks of a careful exploration of snacks

Alexander had always forbidden himself wearing away the hard edges, but still there.

Alexander shivered beneath his touch, and his erection bobbed in his boxers, and Miles had to drag his eyes away.

"Are you going to?" Miles asked, and Alexander bit his lip.

"I don't know," he said, honestly. "Maybe."

"Fuck," Miles breathed, and couldn't help but snake his hand down and beneath the waistband of his boxers, taking a hold of himself. He was already so close, it was going to be quick and dirty, nothing like he'd experienced in years.

"Baby," Alexander said, and moved to tug Miles' boxers down and expose him. "Let me see you."

Miles' erection sprung free, and Alexander took a harsh breath in. He seemed greedy with it, and Miles whimpered under his gaze.

"Still okay?" Miles said, and god, let the answer be yes.

"Still okay," Alexander said, hoarse. "Move, baby, let me see you."

Miles tried to make fluid movements, but his limbs were jerky, his hand shaking around his cock as he tugged at it, moving up and down the length, playing with the slit and the precum there, feeling Alexander's intense gaze on him as he bit his lip and tried to reel it back, to last as long as he could. His eyes drifted to Alexander's boxers, to the way the fabric was staining darker just a little where the head of Alexander's cock was leaking too.

"God, baby," Alexander said, and pushed the heel of his hand against his own cock through the fabric, and he was shaking too, echoing Miles' body with his own, and as Miles sped up, Alexander whined, pushing against the heel of his hand, rocking with it.

"Look at you," Miles breathed, "look at you."

"Miles, baby, I'm going to – " Alexander said, stuttering out the syllables, and Miles goddamn moaned at the broken words, and that was all it took, Alexander went rigid above him, mouth a wide 'o' as he squeezed his eyes shut and the front of his boxers darkened with his release.

Miles watched, felt himself tipping over the edge too, and then he was coming, spurting onto his stomach, eyes fixed on that dark stain and the way Alexander was still kneading his hand against his softening cock.

"Fuck," Miles managed, and closed his eyes, to catch his breath, opening them abruptly as he felt Alexander tracing a finger through the come on his stomach.

Alexander sucked two fingers into his mouth, and Miles could have come again, and his cock jerked a little, spurting once more, and he ached with it, ached with the image of Alexander's fingers in his mouth, tasting him.

"You're going to ruin me," Miles said, husky, low.

"I wanted to know what it tasted like," Alexander said. "I never knew."

"Come here," Miles said, and gestured for Alexander to bend low and kiss him. "It's rude not to share."

Alexander kissed him dirty and all tongue, and Miles could taste himself there, and that was a fucking revelation.

Alexander pulled back, and wriggled slightly against Miles' thighs.

"I haven't come in my pants before," Alexander said, and Miles giggled at him as he tried to peel them off himself without making a mess. "You could have warned me."

"Next time we try it without, huh?" Miles asked, careful to gauge Alexander's reaction. If the flash of heat that went through Alexander's eyes was any indication, it was something Alexander was interested in.

Cock soft and sloppy, boxers pulled down just enough to his thighs, Alexander leant heavy on Miles, seeming not to care about the drying come on Miles' stomach.

"We're definitely doing that again," Alexander said, and it was a promise. "I was scared I couldn't have this with you. But fuck, baby, I want to try everything. You make me lose my mind."

"We've got time," Miles said, hushed, and Alexander kissed him again, softer now, and the taste still lingered, just a little.

"I've got so much to make up for," he said. "I'm glad it was you."

Miles didn't know what to say to that, so he just pulled Alexander closer, careless of the mess they'd made, and held him for a long time, their breathing in sync, Alexander's face buried in the crook of Miles' neck.

*

Falling asleep under the weight of your words

And your arm falls across my hip

You told me to breathe you in

And asked if I could smell her on you

I shook my head because baby

It was only ever you

- *Breathe You In, Miles Montgomery*

*

Miles nuzzled against Alexander's ear.

"Baby, this is lovely, but we really need to shower," he said, and wriggled to prove his point. Alexander made a sad noise in the back of his throat.

"I know, I know, it's one of those things you'll have to get used to," Miles continued. "Do you wanna go first or me?"

Alexander raised his head slightly to look Miles in the eyes, and pressed a lazy kiss to Miles' chin.

"Can we shower together?" He asked, looking hopeful.

"We can," Miles said. "If you feel comfortable with that."

"I want to – try. I liked what we did, what we've done so far. I feel safe with you. And I thought it'd be a good way to figure out where I like and don't like you to touch me," Alexander said, sentences breaking apart as nerves crept into his voice.

"We can do that," Miles said, and smiled, "let's do that."

There was no dignified way to get up and into the shower, but thankfully it was only the room next door, so they made a concentrated effort not to make eye contact as they padded through, morning still light in the air.

Miles set the shower to heat up, and Alexander sat on the rim of the bath, looking at him.

"You looked really good," Alexander said. "When you were – and when you, when you came. I liked that."

"You looked pretty good yourself," Miles replied. "You keep surprising me. Not that you looked good, I could have predicted that, but I like that you can make these decisions for yourself. You feeling okay?"

Alexander considered for a moment.

"Weird. Not bad weird, just weird. Like I got something back that I didn't realise I'd lost. Autonomy? Is that the word?"

Miles nodded, listening intently.

"I think," Alexander continued, "we've not been thinking about anything, have we, outside of this apartment and just surviving day to day? And that's fine, and it works, but it feels like I can allow myself to think about what happened and it feels very far away right now. I know it happened to me - I know it's always going to be there, but when I'm with you, even just looking at you, or giving you shit about the stupid things you say - or watching you make music, it feels like she can't hurt me anymore."

"It's okay, baby," Miles said.

"I know," Alexander said, "and I like this. I like this world we've built. I don't want to leave it. I like London. I want to see more of it. There's so much history here. It's old, you know? I like you, Miles, and I thought before that perhaps I liked you more than I should, but now it feels like I like you just the right amount."

"And you call me a wordsmith," Miles said, and shook his head ruefully. "Baby, I like you too, an insane amount, but you're right, just the right amount. And if you're ready for the world to get bigger, it can. We're not prisoners here. It's been a couple of months now. We're probably safe. Theo and Eiko are coming down on Sunday, you'll get to meet them. Maybe we could do something with them?"

"I don't know, they're your friends – " Alexander said, and Miles shushed him.

"They're going to love you. Theo's like a goddamn Labrador, he'll love on anyone if they tell him he's a good boy. And Eiko's just a sweetheart. Far too good for him, but they're so in love. It's kinda gross, sometimes, to be honest. You don't have to hang out with them, but it's a thing we could do. If you wanted. No pressure."

"I'd like that, I think. I just – I've never hung out with a partner's friends before. It's still all new to me," Alexander said.

"Partner, huh? I like that. Like we should be either solving crimes or committing them. Maybe both," Miles mused. Alexander reached out and pinched his side, keeping him on track. "Okay, sorry, yeah, you look up some things you'd like to do or see, and we'll figure something out. Eiko's really into art museums, if that helps."

"It does," Alexander said. "Doesn't sound too stressful."

Miles checked the water, and was so thankful for the water pressure, which was strong enough that it almost hurt to the touch.

"You want to get in?" He asked, and Alexander nodded.

The shower was easily big enough for the two of them, and they started off inches apart again, as far as the cubicle would allow, before slowly finding their way back together.

"Okay, so we need ground rules," Miles said. "If we're going to start having sex. So neither of us freaks out. There's stuff I don't like too, ya know? So you tell me one safe spot I can touch, and I'll tell you. How does that sound?"

Alexander nodded, and leaned in closer. He touched his fingertips to Miles' hip, nothing sexual, just grounding.

"I don't know if I want you to touch my ass," he said, "not yet, anyway. But you can touch my dick."

Miles nodded, and ran a hand down Alexander's cheekbone, before replying.

"You can touch my ass anytime, but I'd like a warning before fingers or anything. And I like a lot of lube, like so much lube. I'm not someone who gets off on pain."

"I think – I think fingers in my mouth would be okay, but I'm not sure about anything else. I'm scared of choking. And I don't like having my hair pulled," Alexander said, shuffling his feet and drawing away from Miles a little, as though he'd said the wrong thing.

"Baby, that's fine," Miles said. "We can work around that. I like having fingers in my mouth, and I'll happily suck your dick, but I don't like rimming so much. I love having my hair pulled though, but gently. Again, not into the pain thing."

"I like watching you," Alexander said. "I think even if I didn't want to get off, I could still watch you. It feels like you're sharing something with me that nobody else gets to see."

"I like watching you, too," Miles said. "And there's never any pressure to get off. If it happens, it happens. Sometimes, it just doesn't. The journey is all part of it. It's about feeling good, right? So we don't do things that don't feel good."

"I'm still expecting this to be hard," Alexander said. "These past few weeks, you've never pushed me, and I've felt like if anything, I was the one pushing. And you've let me. And I like that, that you let me decide what we do. But I want you to know you can ask for stuff too. And I can say no. I can, now. I know I can say no and you won't be upset."

"There are going to be times when it *is* hard," Miles admitted. "But look at us, using our words. And you can ask me things and I can say no, too. I can be too tired, or just not feeling it, or I don't need a reason at all. And even if we're halfway through something, you can say no at any time and we'll stop. And if you can't find the words to say it, we'll figure something out too. Like, you can pinch me or something."

Alexander reached out and pinched just below Miles' nipple, causing him to splutter indignantly.

"Well, you've got that figured out, at least," Miles complained.

"Thank you," Alexander said, and leant his head against the cool tiles behind him, and Miles moved carefully closer, not crowding, but just enough into his space to press his nose into Alexander's neck and inhale, before pulling back.

"This shouldn't be something you have to thank me for," Miles said.

"It was a bigger thank you," Alexander said, and swept a hand through Miles' wet hair, causing it to stand up before being patted down again by the water. "For everything."

"Well, thank you, too, then. For being you. For being so ridiculously, endlessly, you," Miles replied.

"Can I wash you?" Alexander asked, looking shyly at the shower gel on the shelf, then at Miles, not quite meeting his eyes.

"Yes. Can I wash you, too?" Miles asked.

Alexander nodded.

Miles handed him the shower gel, and Alexander smiled, that small secret smile he only ever shared with Miles.

They washed each other, bodies turning in the humid air, each touch sacred and rooted in a sense of security neither of them had felt before, touching just to touch.

After, they sat on the bathmat, towels draped over them, leaning against one another.

"You're one of a kind, Alexander Raine," Miles said.

"So are you, Miles Montgomery," Alexander replied, and pressed a kiss to Miles' cheek, lingering there for a few seconds, before pulling back. Miles sighed with it.

Chapter Eleven

@RollingStone: New Miles Montgomery album? Theo and Eiko dream team spotted in London recording studio: rollingstone.com/news/miles-montgomery-theo-eiko-london...

*

Miles had noticed. The way Alexander had found a certain comfort in himself, the way he'd settled into a new rhythm. He currently seemed to be obsessed with trying every vegan restaurant in the local area, and he'd steadily worked his way through Jacob's weird bedside library. It was like he was allowing himself to breathe for the first time in years. It heartened Miles to see it. He'd taken day trips to the London History Museum more than once, bringing home huge coffee table books they had no room for but that Alexander found too beautiful to refuse. And Miles couldn't refuse him them, either. He looked like a different man, more casual, dressed down. Happy.

"You don't work out so much now," Miles said, one evening, a few days before Theo and Eiko were due to arrive. He rested a hand on Alexander's abdomen, feeling the slight softness there, a hardiness that hadn't been there before. "You were all sharp edges, and now you're not."

Alexander looked at him, tilting his head slightly in that way he did when he couldn't quite believe Miles was real.

"You don't mind?" He asked, eyes glancing over Miles' face, waiting for the answer.

"This is real," Miles replied, "chest hair and more than two per cent body fat, it's real. How you looked before, it used to scare me a little. For your sake, not mine. I like watching you eat. I like that you don't feel like you have to be beyond perfect all the time."

"I feel safe," Alexander said. "You won't leave me if I'm not perfect. I don't think that's who I want to be anymore. A body. Sculpted. Something to look at."

"You don't have to be," Miles promised.

"I want to go back to school," Alexander said quietly, placing his hand over Miles'.

"What do you want to study?" Miles asked.

"History," Alexander said, after a pause.

"All of it?" Miles asked, and Alexander laughed, and it echoed through his stomach, through their joined hands.

"Yeah, baby, all of it. You know, how to stop it happening again. People – they fuck up over and over. I like when I get the questions right on University Challenge. And I like – I like the idea of being on it, a bit. And maybe – maybe teaching one day. Like, I think I could do that. I think I could be good at it."

"You could, I could see that. You'd be really good at it – you taught me how to set up the wifi, I know that's not the same thing, but if you've got the patience for that, then you can handle pretty much anything as far as I can tell. Damn. I'd never really thought about it. But yeah, we could get you there. Anything you want. You want to look at universities soon?" Miles asked.

"I think so. Not right now, but maybe next year?" Alexander said, ducking his head.

"It's a date."

*

They were due to meet Theo and Eiko, and Miles found Alexander fiddling with the blister pack of pills, something he hadn't touched since they'd arrived in London.

"Baby," he said, resting his hand on Alexander's hip and feeling some of the anxiety drain away through the touch. "It's just Theo and Eiko. I promise you, you'll love them. There's no pressure to be anybody but yourself, okay?"

Alexander put down the pill packet on the side and moved to rest his forehead against Miles'.

"I'm just not sure if I'm ready for our world to get bigger, is all," he said.

"I know," Miles said. "I know. But it has to, right? Not in a bad way. We're going to be working on the album, you've picked out the Tate for us to visit, we might get food, we might not, it's all going to be fine. Look," Miles pulled out his phone and tapped it a couple of times, before showing a messaging string to Alexander. "Eiko's obsessed with seeing the fox cubs. You're going to have to have a sleepover with her. Blanket forts and everything."

"I'm not good at this," Alexander said. "I never was. I had Jacob, and the people around Jacob, and then I had you, but I'm just – what if they're better than me?"

Miles looked at him, the way his eyes were wide and nervous.

"How could they be better than you?" Miles asked.

"I'm – you've been stuck with me for such a long time. What if you realise there are better people out there? What if – " He was cut off by Miles poking him in the side, and he squirmed away.

"No. We're not spiralling right now. I love Theo and Eiko, they're my friends, they're my family. But they're not you. Nobody's you but you. You're Alexander, and I want you around because you're Alexander. Not to be somebody else. Just to be you. You get that?"

Alexander nodded. A small smile appeared on his lips.

"It's just weird," Alexander said.

"What's weird?" Miles asked.

"How much you keep giving me," Alexander replied. "So much of yourself, all the time. And yet you never seem to run out. How do you do that?"

"Because you give it right back, in a thousand, a million different ways. This isn't a one-way street, baby. You save me every time I save you. That's how we work. We keep saving each other," Miles said, and leant into Alexander a little.

"Okay," Alexander said, breathing out, long and slow. "Okay, let's go meet Theo and Eiko."

"You sure?" Miles checked.

"I'm sure," Alexander replied.

"You don't have to be," Miles said, checking in.

"No, it's okay, I want to do this," Alexander said.

"If you want to leave, just like, pinch me or something," Miles said.

"Oh, just give me a reason," Alexander said and grinned.

"You're so brave, Alexander Raine," Miles whispered, just glancing past Alexander's ear. It was the truest thing Miles could have said, barring three words that kept bubbling up under his tongue.

One day, he'd spit them out and let them hover between them. But not yet, not just yet.

*

Theo and Eiko were staying at the K-West hotel, an easy walk away from Jacob's apartment. Miles slipped his hand into Alexander's and nudged his shoulder; easy, grounding contact.

They arrived at the hotel only for a scruffy haired man to launch himself at Miles in a bear hug. Miles briefly saw Alexander raise an eyebrow as Miles tried to lift Theo off his feet and spin him round.

"A romance for the ages," a woman mused, and stepped forward to shake Alexander's hand. "I'm Eiko. You must be Alexander."

Alexander smiled, and shook her hand.

"It's nice to meet you," he said, and glanced over at where Miles and Theo were still hugging it out. "Is this going to take much longer?"

"We can hear you, asshole!" Miles called, and still entangled with Theo, shuffled back over. "Eiko, hi!"

"Hello, Miles," she said, placidly. "Do you mind disengaging from my husband now?"

Both Miles and Theo let out low whines at the thought of it.

"They only make out when they're really drunk," Eiko stage whispered to Alexander, "and even then it's some kind of bizarre bro make out session. It's difficult to describe."

"Babe," Theo said, "that was one time."

Eiko raised an eyebrow.

"Pfft, details. Alexander, this is Theo. I once dared him to eat a worm," Miles said, and Theo grinned crookedly.

Miles briefly marvelled at having some of his favourite people in one room, especially as Alexander's face shot from disgusted to amused.

"Tell me you were a child at the time," he said, and Theo shook his head.

"Whatever you wanna hear, man."

"This guy," Miles slapped Theo on the chest, a gesture borne from years of friendship. "Is going to help me make the best fucking album in the world."

Eiko cleared her throat.

"And Eiko is too, because Eiko is amazing and we all love Eiko," Miles quickly added.

"Is it too late to fly back to America?" Eiko said to Alexander, who grinned, and Miles could see the way she put him at ease, her quiet humour and congeniality both a balm against the anxiety of meeting someone new.

"I'm wondering the same thing," Alexander replied, and Miles huffed.

"Traitor," he said.

Miles watched Theo sidle up to Alexander and look him over, and Miles wondered if he was taking in the way Alexander had nervously changed his clothes three times before leaving the house or had fussed with his hair for half an hour in the mirror. He'd been so desperate to make a good first impression. He seemed to like what he saw, because he nodded before holding out a hand for Alexander to shake. Alexander took it, and it seemed only Miles noticed the slight sharp inhale of breath as Theo drew him into a quick bro hug, even as he awkwardly patted Theo on the back.

"So you're the guy Miles has decided to write a dozen songs about, huh?" Theo said, and Miles tried really hard to be nonchalant about the fact that, yes, Alexander was, and Theo knew exactly what that had to mean.

"Apparently so," Alexander replied evenly.

"Dude, it's going to be so rad, you don't even know. Best album yet. All the awards. We're going to strip it right back and let your boy fuckin' shine. You have no idea," Theo promised.

Miles watched something akin to pride push its way across Alexander's face, even as the whirlwind that was Theo seemed to blow him away slightly.

"As exciting as this all is, I don't think the proper place to discuss it is a hotel lobby," Eiko interjected. "I believe I was promised food?"

Miles couldn't help but grin. These were his people. He couldn't have comprehended how much he'd missed them until he didn't anymore.

"Food you shall have," he said easily.

They stepped out onto the London streets, Miles and Theo walking beside each other in front, Eiko and Alexander a quieter couple behind them.

The promise of the album bubbled under Miles' skin as Theo launched into grand ideas and thoughts about arrangements.

It was exciting, but there was only one person Miles really cared about hearing the album, and glancing back over his shoulder, he smiled as he saw Alexander with his head bowed, listening to Eiko talking quietly.

Alexander had said Miles wrote about what he loved, unapologetically.

Well, this album felt truer to that than any other.

Which was terrifying, but in a really good way.

*

Being back in the studio reminded Miles why he had gotten into this in the first place, all those years ago, back when he'd been all colt-like limbs and hopeless optimism. Bouncing off Theo and Eiko's ideas, fighting for lines he needed to keep, and killing his darlings, squirreling lyrics away for another day, hearing the synth lines Theo had put together while he and Eiko had still been in America, seeing the string section arrive and elevate what had been chords he'd plucked out on that old acoustic guitar, it made his heart swell and reminded him that this, this glorious act of creation, was the reason he was alive, why he did all of this, why he'd put up with so much for so long.

He grinned across at Theo, who grinned back, reaching out a hand and slapping Miles on the shoulder.

"This is good, right?" Miles asked, and Theo just scoffed, like it was obvious.

"Best fuckin' thing you've ever made, you better keep him around," he replied.

They hadn't really talked about Alexander. Theo knew more than most about Miles' dating history, he'd practically been a therapist during some of the previous albums' recording sessions, helping Miles arrange songs into something that didn't make him cry to sing them. Theo had taken Miles out drinking after those late nights, turning into early mornings, drowning old sorrows and new.

This felt different though. Miles wasn't eulogising someone this time, he was celebrating. This wasn't a wake, this was a party.

Not that every song came easy, and without its hiccups. Maybe the media was right when they talked about Miles always leaning into the darker subject matter, the nasty bits, like a scab he couldn't help but pick at. Songs like *New Jersey* felt like an open wound the first time he laid down the vocals, and he'd come home to Alexander and just held him, shaking at the memories they both shared, sorry that it had happened, except not sorry at all, because the world had led them to this point.

There'd been discussions, so many, and Miles had pored over the lyrics with Alexander, scribbled down or typed up in his phone, checking over each verse to make sure they were okay. Alexander, Miles had made certain, had ultimate veto power over every fucking word, and to his credit, Alexander used that power with a responsibility Miles envied.

"You have to tell the truth, baby, but can you just change that line – just the way you sing that is too close to what she said to me," Alexander had said, one night, as they'd both stared at

Miles' phone and he'd sung the melody under his breath for what felt like the millionth time. "We do this right, okay?"

"I don't want to hurt you," Miles had replied.

"I won't let you," Alexander had said, as though hurt was something he could avoid, something he trusted Miles to help him avoid.

He was fair in a way Miles wasn't sure he could have been in the same situation, as Miles pulled them apart and put them back together again.

"This isn't a break-up album," Alexander reminded him. "There won't be a break-up album."

God, Miles had to tell him soon. The three words that bubbled on his tongue and made him weak kneed and delicate to the touch. Every time Alexander touched him, innocent or otherwise, he wanted to whisper it, scream it, a thousand different ways to exclaim that it was *love*, burning him up and making him whole all at once, and he didn't know how to feel so full and not explode with it.

There was a song Alexander didn't know about explicitly, a song Miles had written lines for but hadn't put together cohesively, a song Miles had pulled Eiko aside to work on, because whilst he appreciated Theo's input, Eiko had a softer touch, and a more introspective one. *Alexander's Song* was the love letter Miles had been trying without meaning to, to write since the first day he'd met Alexander, and the title wasn't original, but it didn't need to be. It would be the song that closed out the album, the song that would stay in people's heads the longest, the song where the string section got quiet and low and hummed along to the words Miles was singing, Eiko's piano playing in the background, her harmonies matching his and swelling into something that was utterly undeniable.

Miles loved Alexander, and he couldn't deny it, and he didn't want to.

What made him feel untethered, as if he could drift away was that he was pretty sure Alexander felt the same way. Because in the same way Miles had had to stopper his tongue, he'd seen Alexander doing it too, the way sentences had ended abruptly, so much left unsaid.

The album was put to bed three short weeks after Theo and Eiko had flown in, but not before Eiko had approached Miles with an idea, something that reminded him why he loved her so much.

"We can make this a double album," she'd said. "These songs deserve to be sung live. You, me, Theo and a string section. We can make it happen. I've been looking at venues. We could record it. Sell tickets for charity. Let's do something new. This is, after all, something new, isn't it?" She'd smiled knowingly, and Miles knew she was watching the gears in his head start to turn.

*

"It's going really well," Miles said to his father, phone wedged between his shoulder and his ear, scribbling idly on a notepad. Alexander was in the shower, and Miles was half focused on Homes Under The Hammer on the television. "Yeah, it's nearly done now, I think. Just some last minute fiddling, I think. You know how I get."

"I do," his father said. "Now, about this Sink woman. I know you don't want to talk about her, but I wanted to update you. We've got all the evidence we need to bring this to trial, I need you to talk to Alexander about whether he wants to be a witness."

"Dad, you know I'm not going to ask him to do that," Miles said. "He doesn't even know I told you about her."

"You shouldn't keep secrets like that, kid," his dad replied. "It doesn't do any good."

"He's not going to find out," Miles said. "It's better if he doesn't know. It's all – trauma stuff. He's getting better. He's hanging out with Eiko, they're like, best buddies now. And we're doing really good, too. I think he's it for me, y'know? I don't want to ruin that. Not with the whole – past shit."

"You might have to," his dad said.

"Nah, I'm good. Look, I've got to go, but love you."

"Love you too, kid. Be careful."

"Always am, bye."

Miles hung up the phone and startled when he looked up to see Alexander in the doorway, clothes clinging damply to him. Alexander's face was closed off, exactly the same as it had been the night Miles had first met him, standing stock still, body language betraying nothing.

"You told your dad about me?" Alexander asked, his voice small. "I thought – I didn't think – I thought that was going to be – ours."

"Baby," Miles said, standing and reaching out. Alexander flinched backwards. "Baby, no. It was – after you told me and I just wanted to do something, anything. I was trying to protect you. I didn't tell him anything bad. Not anything you said. Just what he needed to know."

"And you didn't think *I* needed to know that?" Alexander asked, angry now, every syllable cutting like a knife.

"No - yes! I don't know! I thought it'd hurt you - and obviously I was right, because now you're upset!" Miles said, words whirling out. He'd done the right thing, hadn't he? He was sure he'd done the right thing. He hadn't fucked up. Not this time.

"Because you lied to me, Miles, we're not – we aren't supposed to do that. Not to each other. Jesus Christ, I'm supposed to be able to trust you. More than anybody else. If I can't trust you, who the fuck do I have? What else have you lied about? Have I still got you?" Alexander's breathing was ragged, like his lungs were being strangled.

"You've still got me!" Miles protested.

"Not if you're keeping secrets from me, Miles – fuck!" Alexander ran a hand roughly through his hair. "I can't stay here. Fuck." He looked desperately around the room, looking for all the world like a cornered animal.

"Don't leave," Miles begged, the words feeling too small on his tongue and his tongue feeling too swollen in his mouth as he swallowed back tears. "Please, just stay."

"I can't – I can't be here right now, Miles," Alexander said, already tugging on his boots, fingers fumbling the laces.

"Where are you even going to go?" Miles asked desperately.

"I don't fucking know, okay? I'm just going to go," Alexander gritted out, trying to get the door open.

"You haven't got your phone!"

"I don't care!"

Alexander slammed the door behind him and Miles listened to the footfalls as he crashed down the stairs before they faded and the silence began to ring. He thought about following for a moment but it felt like he might actually collapse. Instead he just stood, shaking in the middle of the room.

"Fuck," Miles said, then louder, "*fuck.*"

*

Miles paced for a long time, before curling up on the couch and mindlessly watching television, flicking between channels before settling on some stupid panel show repeat. Alexander's jumper was still flung over the back of the couch and it was all Miles could do not to snuggle into it. The audience laughter washed over him as he felt the tears plop down the sides of his face and into his ears. The hours passed, and the sky grew darker and darker until the street lights outside flickered on. He'd almost given up hope when the apartment buzzer went, and with shaking legs, he moved to answer it.

"Alexander?"

"I really don't want to talk to you right now, but can you let me up?"

"Yeah."

He buzzed Alexander up, and a few moments later, he was at the door, looking somehow so much smaller than usual. Miles desperately wanted to hug him, but he knew he couldn't, not right now.

Alexander looked at him and shook his head, hands in his pockets, foot scuffing the welcome mat outside.

"I really want to hate you, Miles," he said.

"That'd be easier, huh?" Miles agreed.

"Don't joke, Miles, not right now," Alexander said, voice heavy. He stepped past Miles into the hallway, and they stood there opposite each other, unsure where to go from there.

"I'm not. I've done this before. Believe me when I say that for everyone involved, it's usually easier to hate me."

"Then I guess it really would," Alexander said and sighed heavily. "Wouldn't solve anything, though. You're sleeping on the couch tonight. And fuck, you're not keeping any more secrets from me, okay? I can't deal with that. I'll leave. I don't know where I'll go, but I will leave."

"I need to tell you something then," Miles said, and watched as Alexander's face turned pale. "No, it's a good thing this time. I promise."

"You promise?" Alexander said, voice nervous.

"Yeah. There's this song – "

*

It was just gone two and Miles was tossing and turning on the couch when a shadow appeared in the doorway.

"The bed's too big without you," Alexander said quietly into the darkness. "I didn't realise beds could be too big."

Miles struggled to untangle himself from the nest of blankets he'd wrapped around himself.

"Alexander, I – fuck. I'm sorry."

"Can we not? Just, I was laying there, and the foxes are out. They're bigger now. They're not cubs anymore. I thought we could watch them for a little while. Just – can we just do that?" Alexander asked, reaching out a hand tentatively.

"Why are you being nice to me?" Miles asked, letting Alexander help him up.

"The world doesn't end just because you fucked up, Miles. If you treat me like glass, then you will make me break. So don't make me break, Miles. Just – use your damn head sometimes. I care about you. A lot. Probably more than I should. Now come watch some foxes with me."

Alexander pulled Miles to his side, body heat against body heat.

"We're good?" Miles asked, voice small in the darkness like it might disappear entirely.

"We will be," Alexander replied.

*

"I know you don't have a title for the album yet," Alexander said, as Miles sprawled on the couch, his head in Alexander's lap, letting Alexander pet his hair. "Eiko and I were talking. The night you stayed late at the studio and she stayed over. The fox cubs were playing, and I remembered what I'd told you about them being trickster spirits. Turns out, she knew more than I did. She said something, I don't know if I'm pronouncing it right, *kitsune*, it means fox spirits. And I thought – I thought back to the night I kissed you, and how I could hear them screaming in the background, and I knew they were playing, but god, in that moment, I could have believed I was possessed with how much I wanted you. It's just an idea, but I wanted to mention it."

"Terrible, brilliant man," Miles said, lifting a hand to stroke vaguely at Alexander's face, narrowly avoiding putting a finger up his nose as

Alexander squirmed away. "And terrible, brilliant Eiko. You two don't need me at all, do you? You've got it all figured out."

"You like it?" Alexander asked.

"You gave it a name," Miles replied. "You found its name. Yes, I like it, duh."

"I'm glad," Alexander said, and Miles shifted so that he could bury his head into Alexander's stomach, mirroring that first night Alexander had slept with his face pressed against Miles'.

"Don't stop stroking," Miles mumbled. "Terrible, brilliant man."

"Only for you," Alexander said, and kept stroking Miles' hair back. "You need to know that. Only for you."

Chapter Twelve

Miles found out he owned his music again three months after the phone call from Jennifer where she'd told him he was haemorrhaging. Financially, he'd been decimated by it, but it didn't matter. He pulled Alexander close and nipped at his bottom lip, letting Alexander squirm against him and try to find friction.

Miles blew Alexander, sloppy and dirty, pulling out every trick he'd ever learnt.

"If this is how you always respond to good news, I'm definitely going to keep you around," Alexander had murmured, after lazily jerking Miles off, wringing his orgasm out like he wanted it to last.

Miles laughed, long and hard, until his belly ached with it.

"You have no goddamn idea," Miles said, and poked Alexander in the cheek, letting Alexander chase after his finger with his tongue.

The world was shifting, becoming something new, and they were shifting with it, evolving, changing. They weren't who they'd been all those months ago in that Brooklyn bar, and Miles found it hard to imagine ever being that person again.

"This is real, isn't it?" He asked, thinking aloud.

"It's real, baby," Alexander replied, and gathered Miles close, nose brushing against Miles' too-long hair. "Impossible, but real."

*

Woke up at 3am and knew that you'd be there

Didn't know what I was asking for

Something like a prayer

All the gods and all the demons

And all the mischief in between them

Rip me to shreds, rip us into pieces

Watch you become someone else just long enough to blink

But I found ocean eyes and they reflected me back

I found my way through a twenty year heart attack.

- *New Jersey, Miles Montgomery*

*

milesfuckingmontgomery.com

*Miles is proud to announce his upcoming album **kitsune**, and a special live recording at The Barbican in London, UK. Tickets will be allocated via charity raffle, to enter, please click the link below. All proceeds from raffle ticket sales will go directly to charities supporting people who have survived abuse and trauma.*

Click here to enter.

*

BUZZFEED: Miles Montgomery is back, and he is fully out of fucks to give!

*After disappearing off the face of the earth, Miles Montgomery is back, rebranded and with a new attitude and a new boyfriend to write about. Teasing songs with titles like Poor Little Rich Boy and Boots In My Bath, we're all hyped here at Buzzfeed to see what's in store for his upcoming album, **kitsune**. Not only that, but he's offering the once in a lifetime opportunity to see him perform at an intimate venue in London, (tickets available here) where a live version of* *the album will be recorded in front of a lucky few.*

Scroll down for a few of our favourite Miles moments, and click <u>here</u> for our retrospective of Miles' six previous albums (which one made you cry the most?).

*

kitsune track listing

1. poor little rich boy
2. breathe you in
3. one-sided
4. new jersey
5. two hands
6. like you the right amount
7. boots in my bath
8. blanket forts
9. orange juice
10. miss me
11. messy
12. trick
13. nice
14. alexander's song
15. (barbican secret sessions hidden track)

*

With his guitar strapped to him, and swung behind his back, his white t-shirt proudly declaring **WHO THE FUCK IS MILES MONTGOMERY** in bold black letters, Miles stood at the side of the stage, the lights down low, looking into Alexander's eyes, feeling the weight of Alexander's hands loose on his hips.

"You're going to be amazing," Alexander murmured.

"I'm scared," Miles replied.

"I'll be right here, baby, the whole time," Alexander promised. "Now go be a rock star."

Miles stepped onto the stage.

*

BARBICAN SECRET SESSIONS RECORDING TRANSCRIPT

MILES: *This song is, uh, about Buzzfeed. [laughter] No, it's about fame and how people turn on you sometimes. It's a lot of fun. It's called Poor Little Rich Boy. We have a string section, just in case you need someone playing the world's smallest violin. Okay, we ready to go? Let's do this.*

MILES: *Okay, I'm joined by my best friend Theo on guitar and his beautiful, amazing, fantastic wife Eiko who is far, far too good for him on piano. And we have, as previously mentioned, a string section, because we're just that pretentious. Okay, this one is called Breathe You In, and it's about – it's about when someone thinks you can only see the people they were before they became the person they are now. We're all – changing all the time, and this is about that.*

MILES: *Wow, okay. Erm, so when I first met my partner, we talked a lot, and it was weird, because I kept thinking to myself, what if this is one-sided? And when you're in a relationship, there are always two sides at first, but in the end, you become this united front, and so this is One-Sided, because in the end you're both on the same side.*

MILES: *This song is called New Jersey. It's about – well, you can guess. But it's also about really seeing someone for the first time and feeling so alone in the world except for that person. And yeah – it's a lot. Let's just do this.*

MILES: *So when I was a kid, I didn't understand the phrase 'one hand clapping' and I thought it must mean something rude. [laughter]*

And that kind of stuck with me, and like, sometimes there can be two hands, attached to two different people and, ha, yeah, that's what this song is about. Oh my god. This is Two Hands.

MILES: *Okay, we survived that. Sorry, my partner, he knew about that one, he thinks it's hilarious, I swear. He knows about all of them. Well – I mean. You'll see. But erm, anyway. This one is about realising you like each other the same amount and you've stumbled into something really fucking cool and you're in too deep, but you're both in too deep, so it's like you're keeping each other afloat? So it's cool? This is Like You The Right Amount.*

MILES: *Hmm, so I think, I started this when I was seventeen, you know? So it's been over ten years. And I've gotten used to a lot. I've felt used a lot of times. And I've never really spoken up about it. I couldn't. But I could do it for someone else. So this is – this is about being at your most vulnerable and feeling safe because the person you lo- like the most is there with you. This is Boots In My Bath.*

MILES: *So I think love comes in a lot of different forms. And I think you can come back to people who you might have wronged. You* *grow up, you know? And you end up building blanket forts with them at 3am when you're both freaked out because the world is just – so much. So yeah, this is a song about friendship and it's called Blanket Forts.*

MILES: *Aww, you liked that one, huh? Me too. Okay, so I was sitting at a bar drinking orange juice and this guy comes up to me and like, somehow manages to do the opposite of asking me out. And it's just the weirdest thing to happen to me. And I guess he stuck with me because, well. Anyway, this is Orange Juice.*

MILES: *Yeah, it's a bop, right? I think that's my, like, dancey one for the album. Sorry for making it so awkward to request, should have definitely thought that name through. Okay [sighs] this one is about my mom. She died when I was eight years old, and I haven't really spoken about it, and I'm not going to now, except that she forgot me. And I didn't understand what that meant when I was eight years old. It's, uh, it's really hard to comprehend even now. But I loved her so much. I love her. Present tense. This is Miss Me, because I like to think she did, even if she didn't realise who she was missing.*

MILES: *Oh no, don't cry! And hey, I'm not crying, it's – it's fine. Okay, we'll have a little cry. [sniffles] This next one is cute though, I promise. It's about finding the person who is going to see you at your ugliest and you're going to see them at their ugliest and you could walk away at any point, but you choose not to. And you could, but you don't. It's about the act of choosing to stay. This is Messy.*

MILES: *So, the album name is kitsune, and it's based on these fox cubs me and my partner saw playing when we first arrived in England. And one of them played a trick on another one, and I thought – I didn't realise they could do that. So that's where the album name comes from, as well as this song, I guess it's about – it's about sharing that moment with someone and just remembering that it's still possible to laugh. This is Trick.*

MILES: *So my English teacher, at school, always said 'never use the word nice, it's a really boring word', and that really stuck with me. And then, like, falling for someone, there's a lot of really hard stuff, but if you get it right, and if you get lucky, then it's nice. And there isn't a better word for it. It's nice. It doesn't ask anything of itself. I like that. So that's why this song is called Nice.*

MILES: *Right well, this is the last song. And my partner is, yeah, he's looking at me because he didn't know about this one for the longest time. He let me keep it a secret. He trusted me with it. He told me that I write songs about things I love. I do. I want to thank Eiko for helping me keep this one a secret. For distracting him. Because I wrote a song, all these songs, about someone I love. And I kinda wish I could have told him privately, but, well, he knew. He knows. This is Alexander's Song. It's a song about the love of my life. Unless he hates it, in which case [laughter] we'll have a rethink. Oh god. Alexander, I love you. So much. Okay, thank you for indulging me, let's do this.*

MILES: *And I guess, that's the album. I've been Miles Fucking Montgomery. Thank you for being an amazing audience. London, I love you. Thank you. Thank you so much. Good night.*

*

"Do you think they liked it?"

"Baby, you were amazing."

"I'm so tired. God, Alexander I don't even know."

"I love you too, you know."

"Oh shit, I didn't mean to tell the whole world before I told you."

"You tell me every day. Besides, this is who you are. And you are what you love."

"I love you, Alexander Raine."

"I love you too, Miles Montgomery."

"Can we go home now?"

"Yeah, we can go home now."

- *(Barbican Secret Sessions Hidden Track), Miles Montgomery and Alexander Raine*

*

JACOB: *Am I ever getting my flat back?*

MILES: *You're pretentious and I hate you*

JACOB*: I think you're technically trespassing.*

JACOB: *But you did write a song about me so. On this occasion I'll allow it.*

JACOB: *Even though you're an arsehole.*

MILES: *Alexander wants to know if you want to meet up for dinner next time you're over*

JACOB: *Duh.*

*

The Independent: Alexander Raine Says #MeToo

"In an anonymous hotel room in Manchester, I sit with Alexander Raine, former model and partner of Miles Montgomery. Montgomery hovers in the background throughout the interview, moving closer to Raine and squeezing his shoulders or whispering in his ear, gentle reassurances, when things get too heavy. I can't help but remark, afterwards, when Montgomery has gone to pick up coffee, that he's a keeper.

"Yeah, I feel really lucky," Raine replies, and his wording seems at odds with all we've discussed.

But one look at his face when Montgomery walks back in and hands him a muffin, I know he believes it.

Alexander Raine has walked through fire and survived. He deserves a little luck.

After the trial of Samantha Sink, during the course of which we learnt the full extent of –"

END

ACKNOWLEDGEMENTS

Grace – you were the one who received a frantic, fragment of a sentence when this idea hit me over the head and you were the one who encouraged me to write it. You were also the one who then promptly received fifteen unfinished drafts in your inbox all reading "no, read this version" and for some reason, didn't block me. Thank you for walking me through messy relationships and messier commas. I love you, boo.

Jay – you were the one who held my hand through the panic attacks and assured me people don't schedule zoom calls just to yell at people. You're always there for me even when you don't have to be, and I don't know why or how, but you are. A thousand thank yous, always.

Sena – you helped me keep this secret and fully understood my excitement through it all. Somehow you became one of my best friends and also one of my most trusted. You're just really damn cool. Thanks for sticking around. Here's to many more overly dramatic Christmases and birthdays.

Also major shout outs to Reece, Dio, Em, Elanor, Kit, Rosie, Victor and Colleen. Thanks for being the best cheerleaders a person could ask for.

Mikey – thank you for unknowingly lending Miles and Alexander your flat. It's always best to ask for forgiveness than permission, so sorry. They've left a five star rating on AirBNB and have left everything neater than they found it. Thank you for the fox photos that helped spark the whole thing.

Mum – you didn't know about this, I could never find the right time to tell you. This is a win, the win we'd been waiting for for a while. It's my fox book! I bet you never expected me to write a fox book! Thanks for my love of reading and writing, I owe you everything. I love you.

Dad – you'll never read this (thank god) but thank you for my love of music and for trying to teach me guitar so that I could make it sound like I knew what I was talking about. Thanks for taking me to gigs. You're pretty cool, sometimes.

Rosie and the kids – very difficult to write under these conditions, but I couldn't be anywhere else. I love you all so much. Thank you for lighting up my life every day and for giving me a reason to get out of bed.

You, the reader – thank you for sticking with me to the end. Thank you for your kindness to Miles and Alexander. I hope you liked them. I liked writing them. Okay, love you, bye.

Printed in Great Britain
by Amazon